DONNY STEPHENS

A Supernatural/Suspense Novel

BEYOND THE DARKNESS

 **Idea**
Publishing Company

For more information, visit:

www.facebook.com/donnystephens,author

www.donnystephens.com

Publisher: Idea Publishing Company

ISBN: 978-1-7330016-1-8

BISAC: Fiction/Supernatural/Suspense/Contemporary

Cover Design: Chris Lewellyan

Photo and profile image provided by the author

To my devoted readers
Thank you

BEYOND THE DARKNESS

Vintage William Fuld Ouija Board w/planchette circa 1960s

Forward
by Donny Stephens

Spirit boards, as well as other types of mediums such as tarot cards and crystal balls, have and continue to be used as communication beyond our physical realm. The Ouija Board became commonly used as a spiritual means following the Civil War with mediums using it as a divining tool to allow survivors to contact lost relatives. Even though the Ouija Board was first introduced as a parlor game commercially in 1890, it was already the most popular tool of the spiritualist movement prior.

People know not what they do when they venture in the occult; however innocently it seems. By doing so, they open themselves to many spiritual dangers that normally would never occur; one of which is demon possession.

Some demonologists claim a spirit board opens the door to demonic possession, either through the human body or a place, such as a home. Demons reside on what is called the "astral plane", a gateway to the spiritual world, through which spirits travel. These demons, in many cases, have died a violent death, such as murder or suicide and are confused. It is these demons that are said to be attracted to and thus easily conjured through the use of a spirit board. While the talking board remains popular and sold commercially as a "game", it has been attacked by both critics of the occult and those within the occult community who consider it unsafe for this very reason.

I'm certainly not an expert in demonology; I only know what hundreds of sources say and what I've experienced regarding the spirit world. Be assured, that for the many that are misinformed, the spirit board will continue to be accepted as a mere game for entertainment purposes and thus a pivotal device for conjuring up the evil that resides beyond the darkness.

Introduction

Under the dim amber glow of a table lamp, the twenty-five-year-old gentleman worked down his third cigarette of the evening. He sat in his worn, dark green leather recliner, his right leg crossed over his left, eyes focused on the coffee table in the center of the room, his breathing slow and steady, mind wandering on the ten grand he lost forty minutes ago on a bet he never imagined taking with reasonable logic and the odds he faced. Most importantly, it meant his bank account was now empty.

A creaking sound came from the hallway, though he didn't give any attention to it as strange sounds and sights have become the norm inside his home. Instead, his eyes remained fixated on the coffee table, where a spirit board sat unfolded, the planchette resting in the middle. He took a final drag of the cigarette, stifles it, and eased from his chair. Folding the board, he shoved it inside the box with force and placed the top on it.

Under a full moon that peaked over cloudy skies, the man approached the junk shed in the backyard, his trench coat flapping against the gusty winds. He flipped on the light switch and made his way to the back of the shed.

"It is on this shelf," the man spoke, "that you will live out the rest of your life, to never again see the light of day." He placed the board on the top shelf of the shed on a cold October evening in 1954 and never laid his hands on it again.

1

Summer, 1984

Erica leaped from the tailgate. "It's here! Grab my camera!"

David reached inside the truck, taking the 8mm Kodak camera from the middle console. Erica began adjusting the zoom and snapped her first picture of their new home making its way towards them. As the semi-truck began turning sharply to the right to enter the driveway, David ran over to move his truck further back between the pine trees in the backyard. David and Erica stand clear as they watch their first home being positioned down the middle of their yard.

The semi moved into position for the drop. Erica had already snapped a dozen pictures before the trailer home was ready to be blocked up. David and Erica looked on as the movers worked vigorously, placing cinder blocks and concrete pads under the trailer for support. A man shoved blocks underneath, while another helper put them in place. Finally, the trailer was ready to be anchored down. When the team finished, the supervisor and David finalized the paperwork.

David and Erica Chandler step up to the front door and walked into the trailer for only the second time. They had purchased it from a family who wanted to sell quickly. It was not what they had in mind for their first home, but it beat the cramped apartment they were living in.

The Chandler's moved into an old apartment closer to town after getting married in May 1979. When Erica found out she was pregnant, they decided to save up for a place of their own with more room. Nearly five years later, David spotted the trailer for sale in the local paper and after looking at it, the price was incredibly low. With more than enough in their savings, David and Erica signed papers on it just days later.

The feeling of owning a home hadn't set in as they walked through the trailer, tossing around ideas on how to fix the place up. With two bedrooms, two bathrooms, a small laundry room, a decent size kitchen, and a living room it had more than enough space.

Erica stepped into the storage area. She enjoys painting and sees this room as a place to store her painting tools and her easel. The trailer is in fair shape to be ten years old. The carpet in the living room and hallway is lightly stained and worn from foot traffic; the vinyl flooring in the kitchen is beginning to fade in color. In the middle of the living room is a light-colored stain, faint yet still visible. The outdated wall paneling has a few small tears in places. The window treatments consisted of thin white drapes that Erica has plans to replace. The trailer comes with no furniture which gives David and Erica a chance to purchase what they want.

"Wow isn't this great," Erica said. "I can't believe we finally have a place of our own."

"Neither can I," David replied. "I thought we'd live in that apartment forever before finding a place we could afford." David stood in the center of the living room and looked down at the light-colored stain. "It isn't perfect, but it'll do for now."

Erica pulled back the thin drapes, looking out the window. "Such a spacious backyard." She gazed at the old oak tree, with its thick trunk covered in whitish bark and large wide-spreading branches. Acorns blanketed the ground surrounding the tree as it grew along the boundary of the Chandler's backyard.

David walked into what will be little Billy's bedroom. Erica was there also, getting ideas on paint, baby decorations, and all other stuff that sparks a baby's imagination.

"We could put Billy's baby bed over in this corner," Erica said, making motions with her hands. "I was thinking maybe a light blue color on the walls."

"Of course," David said. "I mean, blue is the color for boys."

"Not just that, but I think it would look good in this room."

"I agree," David said, smiling. "Better than pink."

Erica turned to give her husband that sarcastic look that David knows all too well.

"Speaking of Billy," Erica said, "I think we should go pick him up. Pam is probably standing in her doorway, ready to hand him off to us."

"Good idea," David replied. "Let's head out."

As David and Erica leave the house, heading for the truck, David suddenly got an idea.

"You know, we should build a deck."

Erica looked to where David is pointing. "You mean, build a deck off the trailer in the back yard?"

"Sure," David replied. "I've always wanted to build one for us. I helped build dad's deck on the back of his house."

"That's a great idea," Erica replied. "And when you're finished, we can invite some of our friends over and grill."

"Sounds like fun to me. We'll just need a grill and some lounge chairs." David scanned over the small lot, thinking of buying a riding mower for the first time.

As he and Erica began walking to the truck, David looked towards the road, at the wooded area on the opposite side. His eyes are drawn to a beaten trail that leads into the woods, the size of a four-wheeler trail. He looked to his left at the abandoned house that sat on the lot next to them; old patio furniture severely weathered and a barbeque grill standing up against the house remains. Near the middle of the lot stood a small wooden shed. The door was locked.

Erica hopped in the truck as David looked towards his right. A row of grey twig dogwood shrubs, about eight feet tall, separate their lot from the neighbor on the other side. David glanced back at the trail leading into the woods, staring at it for a moment before getting in the truck.

ཀ

David's brother Richard and his wife Pam live in a trailer house that rests on their parent's land. David's only sibling, Richard is three years younger.
Richard and Pam married in April of '83. During the past year of their marriage, the couple has been trying to have a baby, but with no luck.

As David and Erica traveled down the narrow road, David remembers him and Richard as kids, riding their bikes and playing with the neighborhood kids. At that time, David and Richard were the oldest kids on the block so they were looked up to by the other kids, almost intimidating at times. Richard would get into fights with the others and David would have to break them up.

As David and Erica pulled into the driveway, they noticed Pam sitting outside on the front porch with Billy. Richard walked outside with a soda in his hand to meet them.

"Hey bro," Richard said, "have they brought yawl's trailer yet?"

"It's anchored down and ready to move in," David replied. "Thanks for watching little Billy."

"No problem. Pam and I have just been hanging around the house today."

Erica walked up the steps towards Pam. "Billy didn't give you any trouble, did he?" Erica asked.

"You mean this little angel?" Pam replied, looking down at him. "He wasn't any trouble at all. I took him strolling down the road this morning, and then we sat inside and watched Bugs Bunny."

Richard took a swig of his drink. "Yea, Pam enjoys taking care of Billy. I think she gives him more attention than she gives me."

Pam looked at Richard, an eyebrow raised. "Well, that's because you're the big baby."

David burst out in laughter. "Yea, I'd say Pam nailed that one brother."

Richard and Pam get along very well, amid the cruel remarks they make about each other. Unlike Richard, Pam comes from a big family; two older sisters and three younger brothers. She grew up a country girl; being raised on a farm, learning how to cook, and watching her brother's picking cherries from her Adirondack chair on the front porch. Her devotion to family is clearly visible in that she enjoys taking care of Billy and wants to have a child of her own.

Erica stepped over to rub her hand over Billy's head as he sat on the floor, playing with tinker toys. "Thank you so much for watching him for us Pam."

"Sit down Erica," Pam said. "Take a load off your feet for a minute."

"Go ahead sweetie," David said. "I want to run to the junk house and look for that end table I was telling you about yesterday."

"Oh, okay," Erica said as she sits down in a rocking chair, next to Pam.

"You want to join me Rich?" David asked.

"Yea," Richard replied with a grin, "you might need help finding your way out if you get lost."

As Pam and Erica sat outside on the porch talking, David and Richard made their way to the junk house. The small house, just under 300 square feet, contained many items from years past that were handed down through many generations of the Chandler's. David and Richard come from a lower-class family of hard workers; most of them being farmers, others putting years in the local paper mill, and forest industry.

As they looked around the house, they noticed boxes that are brittle to the touch along with years of dust that have settled upon every surface. Richard spotted his first bicycle, hanging on the back wall. David noticed some of his old toys in boxes that are stacked in the back corner. They are unable to get to them for all the boxes and junk laying in the middle of the floor. Numerous boxes of quilts were stacked in the front corner of the house. Before David and Richard's mom passed away, she made quilts during her spare time. Countless hours she would spend in the spare bedroom quilting. It was her favorite pastime. David reached in the box to pull out one of the quilts. He noticed shreds and tears along the edges of the quilts. The boxes had tears in them also.

"I think rats have been in here," David said. "These quilts have been chewed up. And these boxes too."

"I say we set some traps," Richard said. "Catch us a big one."

"Why doesn't dad have these quilts in the house?" David asked. "They're gonna rot out here."

"Mom made a ton of quilts," Richard said. "He keeps her best work in that spare bedroom."

David and Richard began looking around some more. David noticed a box of old paperwork that was almost fully shredded. He shifts through it but nothing important.

"So, you're looking for some table?" Richard asked.

"That old end table that belonged to great-grandma, remember? When you and I were kids, we'd walk by it and she always had an oil lamp and her Bible laying on it."

"Oh, yeah," Richard replied, the memory coming back to him. "it stood next to the fireplace."

"Dad said I could have it if I can find it. He said it was in here somewhere."

The only light they had was from the sun that shined through a small window and the door they left open. Richard shuffled through an old box, where he found his old baseball cards. Since the cards were in plastic sleeves, they were still in good condition.

"Man," Richard said, "I wonder if my ol' Mickey Mantle is still in here."

As David made his way towards the back of the house, he stumbled upon a board game. David reached down to pick it up, wiping off the dust with his shirt.

"What is this?" David asked. "It looks like a board game."

Richard stopped shuffling through his baseball cards to get a look. His eyes widened. "That's a spirit board bro."

"What do you do with it?"

"You ask the board questions and it will slide over these letters and numbers to give you the answer."

"Who does the sliding?"

"That's the magic inside," Richard said with a gleam in his eyes. "It moves on its own."

"I forgot you were always superstitious," David replied, sarcastically, turning back to the board. "It looks old."

Just then, David noticed the end table standing in the corner of the room. "There it is," David said, putting the spirit board down. David removed the boxes that were on the table and walked out of the house with it. Richard followed David outside, carrying the spirit board with him.

"It's just how I remembered," David said as he wiped it down with an old rag. "But without the dust. This will look great standing next to our bed."

"It's nice," Richard said. "Old but nice. Sorry, I'm not really into antiques."

"What about the spirit board?" David asked.

"Take it," Richard said, handing the board over to David. "I wonder where it came from. I don't remember us having it when we were young."

"Neither do I," David replied. "I think I'd remember something that moves on its own."

ॱ

Billy was fully occupied with his toys as Pam and Erica continued talking on the front porch.

Pam stared down at Billy. "Richard and I have been trying to have a baby. I'm starting to lose hope."

"Is there a problem?" Erica asked.

"We've made dozens of attempts, but nothing yet. I don't know if it's me or Richard."

"Have you met with a doctor?"

"I mentioned it casually to Richard, and he quickly said no. He still has hope."

"Well, don't give up. God knows the perfect timing. I'll pray that things work out for you and Richard."

Pam continued to stare down at Billy. "Thanks, Erica. A baby is so precious. It's something I've always wanted."

"They certainly are," Erica replied as she studied Pam, trying to understand how she feels. "You really want a child of your own, huh?"

Pam looks up at Erica. "Desperately."

ᶜ

David and Richard returned to the house, carrying the end table and the spirit board.

"Ready to go, sweetie?" David asked as he put the two items in the truck.

Erica thanked Pam for keeping Billy as she eased from the chair. Pam grabbed Billy, hugging him tightly. "Billy, I want you to come and see me soon."

Billy looked up at Pam. "I will Aunt Pammy."

Pam smiled. "I don't mind keeping Billy anytime Erica. Just let me know."

"I will," Erica said, walking towards the truck with Billy. "Thanks again."

Richard looked at Pam, as she stared at Billy. He recognized a look of sadness in her eyes.

"Are you okay honey?" Richard asked.

"Who me?" Pam replied. "I'm fine. I'll get inside and make us dinner now." Pam eased from her chair and walked inside the house.

David patted Richard on the back. "Talk to you soon brother."

"Yeah bro," Richard replies. "Hey, do me a favor and ask that board if I'm gonna grow up to be rich."

David bent over laughing. "Brother, I don't have to ask the board that question. I already know you're gonna be rich."

"How you know that?"

"Think about it for a minute. See you later Rich."

As David was backing out of the driveway, he noticed Richard laughing and shaking his head. "He finally figured it out."

ᕕ

David and Erica returned to the trailer to drop off the items they found. David took the items inside while Erica watched over Billy as he slept. David placed the end table in their bedroom, in the far corner of the room. He put the spirit board on top of the table and stared down at the box, remembering what Richard said about the board moving on its own. "How is that possible?" he thought to himself.

David picked the box up, looking it over as he becomes intrigued about it. He turned it over to read the directions, which seem simple enough. He looked a little closer towards the bottom corner of the box. It doesn't show a copyright date. David pondered if the board belonged to his dad. He remembered Erica and Billy waiting in the truck and rushes out of the house. As David heads toward the truck, he noticed his neighbor, an old man staring at him through the shrubs. David waved, but the old man doesn't return his greeting, but simply looked on.

"Sorry about that," David said to Erica. "I was just looking at that board game. It's creepy."

"Speaking of creepy," Erica replied, "our neighbor has been staring at us ever since you went in. He was mostly looking at our house."

"That's strange," David replied, looking over at the old man.

"Billy is asleep if you want to go over and say hi."

"Perhaps I should. I won't be long; just enough to break the ice."

"Ok. When Billy wakes up, he'll be hungry, so we need to get to the store."

David stepped out of the truck, making his way towards the man who stood between two dogwood shrubs.

A slight nervous feeling hit David as he came closer to him. David's greeting came out a little choked up. "Hi there," David said, clearing his throat. "How are you?"

The old man tilted his head down as a simple acknowledgment.

"I'm David Chandler," David said, extending his hand.

The old man slowly lifted his hand. "Arthur Rasberry."

"It's nice to meet you, Mr. Rasberry. I believe we'll be neighbors for a while."

Mr. Rasberry replied in a soft, tired voice as if he's suffering from a severe sore throat. He didn't have a tooth in his mouth. "Is that your wife and child?"

David turned toward the truck. "Yes. That's my wife Erica and my four-year-old son, Billy."

Mr. Rasberry continued his stare at the trailer as David catches a hint of suspicion in his eyes.

"Is something wrong Mr. Rasberry?" David asked.

"Where did that trailer come from?"

"It was located about fifteen miles south of town, on Highway 4. Why do you ask?"

Mr. Rasberry took off his worn cap to scratch his nearly bald head. "It's nothing worth mentioning now, Mr. Chandler. I can see your boy is awake now. You have a good day."

David opened the door and fired up the truck. "You ready to go Billy?"

"So," Erica said, "how did it go?"

David turned to Erica before backing up. "I'm not sure."

2

The next two weeks were quite stressful for David and Erica as they prepared to move into their new home. They were so anxious to move out of the tiny apartment they'd been living in for five years, they tried to make the move as quickly as possible. From picking out the furniture to having the utilities turned on, and making cosmetic repairs to the house, they were happy to finally move in. During their strenuous moving attempts, Pam was a big help in keeping Billy for days while they made the transition to the new house.

Throughout the next few weeks, David had built a small deck against the house in the back yard. As David brushed on weatherproof sealer on the last several pieces of wood, he smiled, looking over the finished deck. He wasn't much of a carpenter; spending most of his time working at the local paper mill as a security guard, then coming home to spend time with Erica. He thought of himself as the typical family man; exactly what he wanted in his life. For David, working on the deck was a challenge, but he enjoyed building it. David and Richard would help their father whenever something needed to be fixed around the house. Their father wasn't much of a teacher of trade, thus they had to learn by observation.

As David looked over the finished deck, Erica approached him, smiling.

"Well Mr.," Erica said, "You didn't tell me you were an experienced carpenter."

David couldn't help but laugh. "I'm far from that." He began pointing at a few flaws. "There are some boards not level there and over there –

Erica cut him off with a kiss and replied, "You're my experienced carpenter."

David smiled back and steals a kiss. "I'll accept that."

Erica laughed and stared back at the deck. "How about that housewarming party now?"

ᶜ

The day had arrived. Erica gathered paper plates and cups inside the house, as David cooked on the grill on the backyard deck.

"They're almost done," David shouted.

"We'll have to keep them warm," Erica replied. "We're not expecting anyone for another fifteen minutes."

As soon as Erica got the words out, there was a knock at the door.

Everyone seemed to arrive at the same time; friends of David and Erica's from high school. David and Erica graduated the same year thus a lot of their friends knew each other. About a dozen people had shown up when Richard and Pam arrived. Pam ran over to Billy who was playing in the living room with his miniature cars.

"Billy!" Pam shouted. "It's aunt Pammy!"

Billy held out his hands as Pam grabbed him up. Erica smiled as she watched Pam hold him tightly in her arms. Pam sat him down and looked at Erica. "Let me help you Erica. I'll grab the food."

"Thanks, Pam," Erica replied as she made her way to the deck.

David had a table and chairs set up outside on the deck. David placed the burgers on the table as Erica laid out the vegetables.

There were fifteen people at the housewarming party. Some brought gifts for Erica to open including towels, rags, a 3-piece set of Merry Mushroom kitchen canisters, and a homemade wooden sign that said, "home sweet home". Richard and Pam bought them an Oster "Gold'n Crispy" waffle maker as well as a 10-piece set of colorful Tupperware.

The sun began to set, and the evening was cooling down with a nice calming breeze. The group sat around the grill, staring into the fire that was beginning to fade out. Erica and Pam gathered up the gifts and placed them on the kitchen table inside the house. When she returned outside, the gang were talking about how David and Erica met.

"Why don't you tell them, sweetie," David said, crunching on some chips. "You're better at this than I am."

"I told the story the last time," Erica replied as the crowd waited impatiently. "I told it to your family, remember?"

"I know," David said. "but you can tell it better than me."

After a few seconds, Erica gave in. "Gosh, okay," Erica said, running her hands through her blonde hair. "David and I didn't talk much at school. I mean, we chit-chatted occasionally but that was it. October came around during our senior year and that meant the fair was in town. I went to the fair with my cousin and I remembered playing this game where you throw the ball into that circular thing. You know, the idea is to get the ball in the middle to earn the biggest points?"

Richard nearly stood up. "Whirly points!" he shouted.

David turned towards his brother with a confused look on his face. "What did you call it?"

"Whirly points," Richard repeated. "That's what I always called it."

"It doesn't matter what it's called," Erica said, interrupting. "Anyway, I was playing whirly points and I was having trouble scoring big. I didn't know it, but David was behind me watching my horrible attempt at playing the game. He stepped up and says, *Let me show you how it's done.*" A crummy line I thought, but I stepped aside and gave him a chance. I mean, he seemed to have confidence in himself as he stepped up to the line. Now, I must add, I managed to score just fifty points, but watching David miss every single shot and scoring a grand total of zero, made me feel so much better."

Everyone was laughing, except David. Richard was slapping his knee with his right hand and the other hand pointing at David as if no one in the crowd knew who Erica was talking about.

Erica continued. "Oh, his face was so red. Redder than it is right now. He could barely look me in the eyes he was so embarrassed. But at that moment, I felt something – something I didn't tell him until two weeks later. We spent the rest of the evening at the fair hanging out and listening to a live band. The following Monday, we started hanging out more and the rest, as they say, is history."

"Awe," Pam said, "how sweet."

Erica turned to David, who was looking down and shaking his head. Erica laughed. "Perhaps you'll tell the story next time darling?"

Richard chimed in. "I bet my left leg on it. He'll tell you that he intentionally missed those shots to win your heart."

David looked up, shocked. "Rich!"

Erica turned to David. "Is that true? You made yourself look like a zero to impress me?"

Richard chimed in again. "Yes, he did. From zero to hero!" Richard burst in laughter.

David stomped his foot, staring at Richard. "C'mon that was a secret!"

"Sorry bro," Richard replied. "I couldn't keep it in. It was perfect timing."

Erica sat with her arms crossed. She smiled back at Richard. "Well, I must say he did well. He won my heart and he's certainly my hero."

David turned to Erica with a sexy grin.

"Oh boy," Richard said. "Get a room you too. Pam, we should find the exit and give these love birds some alone time."

Pam replied. "Knock it off Richard. Richard had to make a jackass of himself to get me to fall for him. It involved a 4-wheeler, an amateur driver, and a whole lot of mud."

The whole crew burst out in laughter.

Richard shook his head. "Here we go. I admit I had it coming."

"In due time, my dear," Pam replied. "For now, I'll just say that I'm glad it happened, and I love him so much," Pam added, looking over at Richard.

Richard blew Pam a kiss. "Thank you honey."

◡

As the evening died down and their friends began leaving, David and Erica began cleaning up. Richard and Pam stayed to help. Pam kept an eye on Billy so Erica was able to get things put away. As David was throwing out the trash, Richard mentioned the board game.

David threw the trash into the bin near the road and closed the lid. "I put it in our closet."

Richard replied in a serious tone, "You want to play it tonight?"

"What's with the sudden grave tone in your voice?"

"I'm just asking."

"Well, that's up to Erica. She'll probably say it's getting a little late for board games."

When David and Richard made it back inside, Erica was washing a few dishes and Pam had just put Billy to bed.

Richard asked, "Hey, ya'll wanna play the board game tonight?"

David quickly turned to his brother. "Geez Rich."

"Well, it's kinda late," Erica replied, drying her hands. "It's going on nine."

"This is the perfect time to play," Richard replied. "You don't play this kind of game in the daylight."

"What kind of game is this?" Erica asked, looking concerned at David.

"Bro, you haven't told her about it?" Richard asked with a burst of laughter.

"I haven't had the chance," David replied. "We've been so busy trying to move in. Besides, I don't know too much about it or how it's supposed to work anyway."

Pam walked in from Billy's room. "Richard, you're gonna wake Billy with all that loud talking and ridiculous laughing."

"Well," Richard said, "there are four of us here which is perfect for playing this game. Let's play with it for a minute. I want to see if it moves on its own."

Erica stared at Richard as if he'd officially lost his mind.

David smiled as he stared back at Erica. "The look on your face is priceless right now."

Erica replied, "There's no board game I've ever heard of that moves on its own. It's impossible."

Richard's face turned serious, his tone somber. "You willing to test that belief?"

Erica turned to David who just shrugged his shoulders.

Pam replied, "Well if we're going to do this, count me in on this crazy train."

Richard, Pam, and Erica gathered around a small square wooden table as David retrieved the spirit board from the bedroom closet. As David made his way into the living room, Pam and Erica were exchanging small chit chat about Billy, while Richard was rubbing his hands together in anticipation of playing the game. David set the box in the center of the table and lifted the top off to reveal the spirit board, folded inside. He unfolded it in the center of the table. Everyone went silent…staring down at the odd look of the board.

Erica looked up at David. "Ouija?"

Richard chimed in. "It means good luck."

Pam scoffed. "From the way that board looks, I don't see any good in it."

"You scared?" Richard asked, with a scary-looking smile across his face, almost clownish in appearance.

Pam stared at Richard. "Huh, I am now."

Along with the game was a wooden triangle-shaped piece called a planchette. In the middle of the planchette was a round hole cut out for viewing the letter or number that it slides over.

The board was unique – made from hardwood with graphics printed directly on the board. Letters and numbers as well as a picture of a sun in the top left corner and a half-moon in the top right corner. With the sun, *yes* is printed next to it. With the half-moon, *no* is printed. The word

BEYOND THE DARKNESS | 19

goodbye is printed at the bottom center of the board. The board had square corners and was rough along the edges. David lowered his head to smell the distinct scent coming from the board, reminding him of the antique stores he, Richard, and their father visited down south near New Orleans years ago.

"Richard," David said, "you remember when dad took us to New Orleans when we were younger?"

"How could I forget?" Richard replied exhaling deeply. "There were some wild women down there bro."

Erica turned sharply to David. "Wild women!?"

"Mister," Pam cut in at Richard with daggers in her eyes, "the next thing out of your mouth could get you in some serious trouble. You think this board is dangerous?"

David shook his head. "Knock it off girls. Richard is nuts. We never saw any wild women."

Richard replied, "I read the newspapers when we were down there. They don't lie."

"Oh boy," David said. "Rich, I'm talking about the antique store's dad took us to."

"Oh yeah. I remember those."

"Stepping into one of those antique stores, I smelled a weird scent. I told you about it. How it made me queasy?"

"Yeah, I remember that."

"I smell a little of that scent on this board."

Richard looked down at the board, then at David. "You 'bout to blow chunks, bro? Let us know so we can get out the way."

David rubs his forehead. "Lord help me."

Pam chimed in. "Lord help us all."

"Ok," Erica said, waving her hand at all the craziness. "Let's just play before we lose our minds here."

David pulled up a chair between Erica and Pam. Everyone took glances at each other, waiting for someone to make the first move. Richard set up the board and placed the planchette in the middle.

Richard began. "It's said that all players must place their fingertips on the planchette and move it around in circles on the board," Richard said in a low tone of voice.

"Why?" Erica asked.

"It's called warming up the board," Richard replied. "This board hasn't been played in years. I think we should do it."

"As corny as it sounds, let's do it," David said.

All four players placed their fingertips on the planchette and began moving it in circles on the board. They spun the planchette around for a minute or two, then David removed his fingers. "Ok, that's enough warming I think."

Richard began to introduce the board to the others. "The game is simple. We'll place our fingertips on the planchette, someone will ask a question, and we'll let the board tell us the answer. It will slide over letters or numbers as we keep our fingers lightly on the planchette. It's that simple."

Pam replied, "You mean someone is moving this thing?"

"The board is moving it honey," Richard said. "I told you about this yesterday. The board moves on its own."

"Well, I don't see how," Pam said, getting disgusted. "It's just a wooden piece – nothing mechanical." Pam picked up the planchette, looking underneath it.

"You're overthinking it," Richard said. "Just play the game. You'll see."

They scooted closer to the table and placed their fingers on the planchette that sat in the center of the board.

"Wait," Richard said, getting up from the table and turning off all the lights except the hallway. "It needs to be dark while we're playing. We'll get better responses this way." Then Richard returned to the table.

Pam rolled her eyes. "This has got to be the silliest thing I've ever heard."

"David," Richard said in a whispery voice," why don't you ask the first question."

David looked at his brother, who seemed to be all in this. "What kind of question, your majesty?"

"A general question for now," Richard replied. "Don't make it too hard for the board just yet."

"Oh, my Heavens," Pam said. "Yea, we wouldn't want the board busting a blood vessel from thinking too hard."

"Okay," David said. "Here goes nothing." David took a deep breath. "Are you with us here right now?" David seemed to think that was a simple enough question.

The planchette sat still, not moving an inch. David looked at Richard. "Do you think it heard me?"

"Bro, you're not taking it seriously. We have to focus."

Erica replied, "I agree with Pam. This is crazy."

Everyone took their hands off the board.

"Look," Richard said, "we need to focus and breathe. Closing our eyes will help us relax."

"This is a séance, isn't it?" Pam said. "You've dragged us into some voodoo shenanigans here. Richard, of all things."

"This isn't voodoo Pam," Richard replied. "It's a board game."

Erica spoke up, "Let's keep it down a little. I don't want Billy knowing about this. He's asleep."

Richard placed his fingers on the planchette again. "Let's try again."

David, Erica, and Pam followed suit. After a moment of peace, focusing on their breathing, eyes closed, David asked the question again. "Are you with us here right now?"

Five seconds later, the planchette began creeping across the board, at a steady pace and fell off the board and onto the floor.

Pam jumped from her seat. "Please tell me someone moved it."

"Pam," Richard spoke softly, "sit down."

"I will not sit down until someone confesses," Pam replied.

"Pam, remember what I said to you about the board yesterday and I mentioned that there was magic in this board?"

Pam looked at her husband in a confused state. "I thought you were telling me stories. You do that all the time. I don't know when to take you seriously."

"Take me seriously. Take me seriously," Richard said. "Sit down and let's keep going."

"Why did it slide off the board?" David asked.

"We're not concentrating enough," Richard replied, picking up the planchette. "Let's try it again."

They placed their fingers back on the moving object. David asked the same question and again, the planchette slid off the board.

"Someone's not concentrating," Richard said.

"Well," Pam replied, "how can anyone concentrate when you got a wooden piece moving by itself all over the place? Hell, you know how I feel about all this demonic ritual stuff."

"This has nothing to do with demonic rituals," Richard said. He picked up the planchette, placing it on the board. "Let's place our fingers on it and concentrate before asking the questions. This time bro, ask another question."

The four placed their fingers on the planchette and for a few minutes, they concentrated on it. Then, David asked a different question. "How many are here in this room tonight?" The object began to move; it slid over to 4. Everyone looked at each other in amazement.

"Someone moved it," Pam said, staring at Richard. "And it sure as hell wasn't me."

Erica shook her head. "It certainly wasn't me."

"Rich?" David said.

"Don't look at me bro," Richard said. "I'm not the one moving it."

Pam turned to her husband. "Let me guess. Magic?"

"Exactly," Richard replied with a snarly grin.

"I don't understand how it moves on its own," Erica said, studying the board.

"It's said," Richard replied, "that we are moving the object unconsciously instead of the board moving it."

Pam replied, "That makes about as much sense as carrying a sack of groceries and pushing a shopping cart at the same time. Who told you that?"

"I read about it once in a supernatural magazine," Richard replied. "It was an article on contacting the spirit world. It said that the spirit board was a primary way of contacting deceased entities who have not crossed over or made the transition to the other side."

Pam looked over at David and Erica. "You see what I have to put up with?"

"It's true," Richard said.

"Okay, okay," David said, interrupting. "Let's finish playing. We're already this far into it."

The four placed their fingers back on the planchette. Richard wanted to ask a question now.

He cleared his throat. "Is my old gumball machine in the junk house?"

Pam shot a glance at Richard. "Really?"

"Shhh," Richard said.

They concentrated on the board as the planchette moved over to *yes*. Richard clapped his hands in excitement. "I know where I'm gonna be tomorrow morning."

Pam chuckled. "Yea, at work."

"Crap!" Richard said in disgust. "I'll call in sick."

"O no you are not," Pam replied. "That gumball machine will be right there when you get off."

"Let me ask a question," Erica said, looking at everyone for approval.

"Go ahead sweetie," David said.

The four placed their fingers on the planchette and began to concentrate, waiting for Erica to ask a question.

"What day of the week is it?" Erica asked.

Slowly, the board spelled out *Saturday*.

"What month of the year is it?" Erica asked.

The board spelled out *June*.

"What age is David right now?" Erica asked.

The board slid over *2,* then *5*. David's eyebrows lifted.

"That's 25!" Richard said.

Pam replied, "Listen to Captain Obvious over here."

Erica continued with her line of questions. "Am I older or younger than David?"

The board spelled out *younger*.

"By how many years?" Erica asked.

The board responded *two months*.

"Do I have a birthmark?" Erica asked.

The board slid over to *yes*.

Erica asked a question that no one in the room would know, except David. "Where is my birthmark?"

The board spelled out *bottom center right foot*.

"Wow," Erica said. "That's all correct." Erica turned to David.

"I swear," David said, "I wasn't moving it."

They looked at each other for a moment; all in shock and astonishment.

Pam looked down at the board with conviction, then looked at Richard. "Is it my turn now?"

"Sure honey," Richard replied. He could tell that Pam was about to ask a personal question based on the look she gave him. He was a bit nervous but placed his fingers on the planchette anyway.

After a few moments of silence, Pam asked her question. "Will I ever get pregnant?"

The planchette sat still for what seemed like the longest minute of her life. Pam still had her doubts about whether the board could predict future events. But after the board answered Erica's questions without hesitation and answered them correctly, she had a bit more faith in the board.

Richard noticed Pam's fingers shaking on the planchette. In the back of his mind, he was certain she would've asked this question given the chance. He understood her frustration at trying to get pregnant for the past year. At times, she would blame Richard for them not getting pregnant. But on this night, it never occurred to him that the question would be brought to the spirit board.

The planchette began to move and Richard's heart began racing at the anticipation of knowing what the board's response would be. To Pam and Richard, the board had transformed, within minutes, from a silly board game, into a desperate quest to get answers from someone beyond the darkness.

Pam could barely keep her fingers on the moving object, but it didn't matter. The planchette was moving without her assistance. Richard was hoping it would say yes for Pam's sake, but the planchette moved over to *no*.

Richard looked at Pam, disappointed in the response from the board. "I'm sorry honey," Richard said. "Sometimes the board is wrong."

"Oh," Pam said, almost cutting him off. "Now it's wrong. It answered all of Erica's questions to the T, but it gives me a wrong answer?"

"Just calm down honey," Richard said.

"I want to ask another question," Pam said, turning to the others. "If that's okay with yawl."

With a slight hesitation, the four placed their fingers back on the planchette and began to concentrate. It was a little tough to focus after the board told Pam that she wasn't going to get pregnant. They could only imagine what her next question would be.

Pam sighed, still filled with rage and disappointment. "Am I medically capable of having a child?"

Richard nearly choked on his saliva. Swallowing hard, his heart sank to its lowest as he felt Pam's pain of wanting a child of her own. He knew she was desperate, asking a spirit board for answers. Pam is a skeptic when it comes to spirit boards, tarot cards, crystal balls, and other ways of communicating with spirits. Richard knew that Pam just wanted some relief – she wanted to know that she was going to get pregnant, no matter who or what tells her. He thought about taking his fingers off the planchette, but as soon as the thought crossed his mind, the planchette began to move. The planchette was heading towards *yes* and Pam began to have hope once again. But then the planchette took a U-turn and quickly slid off the board.

Erica spoke up. "Pam, it's just a game. You shouldn't believe anything it says."

Pam looked at Erica, then suddenly rose from her chair, flipping over the table, sending the spirit board to the floor as she stormed out of the house, slamming the door behind her.

"Pam…wait!" Richard said, following her. He turned back towards his brother. "I'll call you tomorrow." Richard left to comfort his wife.

David and Erica stood next to each other, looking down at the flipped table and the spirit board that landed face-up on the floor.

Erica heard Billy crying in his bedroom from all the commotion. "I already hate this board game," Erica said as she walked out of the living room to comfort Billy.

David placed the table on all fours, then grabbed the spirit board, shoving it in the box with force along with the planchette. He put the top back on and back in their bedroom closet.

That night, while David and Erica were asleep in bed, at the stroke of midnight, a cold breeze blew through the house. David woke up with chills all over his body. Sitting up in bed, he ran his fingers over the goosebumps on his arms. He looked over at Erica, who was quietly sleeping. He got out of bed and walked over to the thermostat that was sitting on 76 degrees. It was a cool summer night, but it felt like the temperature in the house was near freezing. Suddenly, David could see cold air as he exhaled. "This doesn't feel right."

3

When the new sewing factory opened just on the outskirts of town, dozens of people flocked over to apply for the new jobs. Erica was one of them. With the short supply of employment opportunities in the quiet little industrial mill town of Jonesboro, most of the population, roughly 5,000, had to drive at least 20 miles for decent work.

The plywood mill, where David has worked ever since graduating high school, is the biggest employer in Jonesboro. The new sewing factory would come in at a close second. The traditional community of Jonesboro got its start when the railroad came through. Once the word was out, hundreds of able-bodied people moved to town, toting hopes of a brighter future. When the plywood mill opened, Jonesboro began to grow at a rapid pace.

As Erica slowly drove through downtown, she noticed the movie "Ghostbusters" was playing this weekend at the Palace Theatre. Erica waved at the elderly folks sitting on sidewalk benches and imagines them carrying on conversations about the unbearable heat that blankets the south this time of year. Erica pulled in at the local pharmacy to pay a bill for when Billy was sick a few months ago. As Erica walked out of the pharmacy, she noticed a flyer on the wall that Herne's department store is having a half-off sale. She wanted a curio cabinet for her and David's bedroom. Not wanting to be the last one interviewed, she made the drive to the sewing factory.

As the line slowly progressed forward, Erica could see what was going on inside the factory. There were two lines of people. Most everyone had their resumes. Erica had previously worked at the local restaurant as a part-time waitress while she was dating David. Her work experience and high school diploma were all she had to go on. She noticed a row of six cubicles, placed together, each one with a curtain drawn. The lady at the desk was announcing that each person grabs an application and proceed to one of the empty cubicles to fill it out and wait for someone to interview you. Erica thought this was a crappy way of getting everyone signed up, but they probably didn't expect this big of a turnout. She knew that she'd be there for a couple of hours at least. Luckily, David was off work today and keeping an eye on Billy.

و

"All right son," David said, sitting down on the couch, "you and I are going to watch the ballgame, ok?"

"Ball aim!" Billy shouted.

"That's right," David said, laughing. "And you know who to root for?"

Billy simply stared at his dad, not knowing how to respond.

"The Atlanta Braves!" David said. "That's our favorite team, ok?"

Billy nodded his head in agreement.

"Who's our favorite team?" David asked.

"Bwaves!" Billy shouted.

"Ata boy!" David replied with a huge grin.

Billy climbed up on the couch next to his dad. Billy's thin blonde hair was all in a mess like he just woke up from a long night of sleep. David reached over and picked up a comb from the end table. "Here Billy, let me straighten that hair out." David combed through his hair. Billy sat there, watching TV, while his dad straightened out the tangles.

"You're gonna be a lady's man when you grow up aren't you?" David said. "Yea, you're not gonna be able to keep the ladies off you."

During the third inning, Billy was down on the floor playing with his toys, tired of watching baseball and wanting to go into his room to play. David walked Billy to his room. "I'll be checking on you by the seventh inning stretch, ok?" Billy smiled up at his dad as if he knew what he meant. David closed his door.

Just then, David heard something crash in the kitchen. David rushed down the hallway and into the kitchen to see one of Erica's favorite casserole dishes shattered in a thousand pieces, scattered across the floor. "Oh no!" David stood there, unable to figure out how the dish could've moved from the back of the counter and onto the floor. After scratching his head and imagining what Erica's reaction will be, he stepped over to the closet and retrieved a broom and dustpan.

e

David waited until that evening before telling Erica about the casserole dish. Erica was exhausted after a three-hour interview process.

"I don't understand," Erica said, standing over the trash can, looking down at the pile of ceramic pieces. "I placed it against the back of the countertop. How could it go from there to the floor?"

"That's what I don't understand," David replied. "That dish was made from thick heavy ceramic. It would've taken someone slamming it down on the floor with enough force to break into than many pieces."

Erica shook her head. "Maybe I can get over to the mall and buy one that's similar. I don't think they make one like that anymore."

"If they do, then we'll find it," David reassured her with a confident smile.

Erica walked over and joined David on the couch. David placed his arm around her as they snuggled in front of the TV. He could tell there was something on Erica's mind. She was quieter this evening than usual. Perhaps, he thought, she was worried about not getting the job at the sewing factory. Or maybe she was upset about losing her favorite casserole dish. Perhaps both.

Erica turned towards David. "Honey, I was thinking maybe tonight we could play the spirit board again."

David craned his head back, surprised. "Why?"

"There's some questions I want to ask," Erica replied.

"Sweetie, you know that board isn't real. It can't tell you what you want to know. It's just a board game."

"Then how do you explain how it moves on its own?"

David was silent for a moment. "Well, I can't."

"What about the questions I asked yesterday? It answered them all correctly. Questions that only the two of us knew."

"I can't explain that either. It wouldn't be rational to say that the board got lucky. There's nothing rational about that board."

"So, can we play it tonight?"

"I thought you hated that board?"

"Well, I do because of how it affected Pam. But I'm still curious."

David chuckled. "You're always a curious one."

"Please David, can we just play it?"

"Well, since you're begging for it, I guess so. But can we make it quick? I have work in the morning you know."

Erica smiled mischievously. "You get the board. I'll set the table up."

With a quizzical look on his face, David went into the bedroom to retrieve the spirit board while Erica put the small square table in the middle of the living room. David returned with the board and positioned it on the table. Erica went to check on Billy before they started. He was asleep. David and Erica sat on opposite ends of the table and placed the planchette in the center of the board. They put their fingertips on the planchette and began moving it around in circles.

David looked up at Erica. "You can begin whenever you're ready," David said.

"I'll start with something simple," Erica said.

David could tell that Erica was very much into the spirit board. He knew that she was fascinated with the supernatural world ever since they first met. During their first few dates, she would ask him questions regarding ghosts and if he's ever experienced one. He told her no. David had never experienced anything ghost-related, apart from some of Richard's made-up ghost stories. David wondered if Erica was a crazy girl who wasn't all there, but she mellowed out greatly and he knew that they would spend the rest of their lives together. Now, here's this spirit board and Erica seems to be all into it. To David, it felt a little unsettling.

Just then, Erica spits out her first question.

"Is my name Erica Chandler?" she asked.

The planchette quickly slides over to *yes*. David and Erica barely had their fingers on it.

"That was a fast response," David said. "It must be alive tonight."

Erica continued with her next question. "Will I get that job at the sewing factory?"

David knew that question was coming. He figured she'd been thinking about it all evening. The planchette slides over to *yes* and Erica looked over at David with a huge grin across her face.

"Now don't get your hopes up sweetie," David said. "Just because some board game tells you it's gonna happen doesn't mean it will in real life."

"I know, I know," Erica replied, taking a deep breath and exhaling.

"Let me ask a question," David said.

"Go ahead honey,"

"Will I retire from the mill?"

The planchette makes its way over to *yes*.

"Well that blows," David said.

"It's just a game, remember?" Erica said, smiling.

"Yeah but with my luck, that'll come true."

David and Erica placed their fingers back on the planchette. "Go ahead, sweetie. I'm done asking questions," David said.

Erica took a deep breath. "Will David and I have another child together?"

David shot a glance at Erica. He didn't think she'd ask such a question. David looked down at the planchette as it moved over to *yes*. Erica's face lit up. Then, without hesitation nor time for a response from David, Erica shoots out another question. "Will it be a boy?" David quickly takes his finger off the planchette that was already in motion.

"Erica, you can't ask that," David said.

"Why not?" Erica asked. "I'm just curious."

"But I'm not. And being curious doesn't give you reason enough to ask that question. It's not a good thing to know the sex of the child before we even conceive it. If we're gonna have another child, I'd rather wait till the right time. I don't want to know that now."

Erica looked down at the board as if coming to an understanding of David's reasoning. "Fine, I won't worry about it since you're gonna be a spoilsport. You want to ask a question?"

"No, I'm good. Are you done?"

Erica smiled, "Just a few more, please."

With a sigh, David placed his fingers back on the planchette with Erica. Erica proceeded with her next question. "Will we be living here in five years?"

The board says slides to *no*.

Erica asked another question. "Will we be living here in three years?"

Again, the board slides to *no*.

David is surprised, but now he's the one that's curious and asks, "Will we be living here a year from now?"

The planchette slowly makes its way to *no*.

David sat confused as he looked at Erica who was also puzzled.

David said, "Give us our home address two years from now."

The board spells out *131 Lincoln Road*; their current address.

"You see," David said, "this board doesn't know what it's saying."

"I don't understand," Erica said.

"It's all mixed up," David replied. "This board says we won't be living here a year from now but tells us we'll be living at this same address two years from now. Let's put it away and go to bed."

"Wait!" Erica shouted, keeping David from closing the board up. "Can I ask one more question?"

"Why Erica? You've already asked it a bunch of questions."

"But not the question I wanted to ask it. Please?"

David straightened out the board and placed the planchette in the middle without saying a word. David gazes at Erica, waiting for her last question.

Erica took a deep breath, the same preparation she gave before asking about their future child. David felt a numbness in his stomach as he awaited her question.

Erica asks, "When will I die?"

David quickly removed his fingers from the planchette and threw the object into the floor for good measure.

"What are you doing Erica?" David shouted.

"I'm just curious," Erica said, reaching for the planchette.

"You can't ask a question like that. Are you crazy? Who wants to know when they're gonna die?"

"I just wanted to see what it says."

"So, what if it says some date this year? Are you gonna be paranoid about it until then?"

Erica shrugged her shoulders. "Maybe."

David shook his head in disbelief at how his wife was acting. "I can't believe you would ask that."

"So, you're not gonna let me ask the question?" Erica said.

"No, I'm not. We're saying goodbye to this board. I think your curiosity has got the better of you."

Erica wanted to continue playing, but she got up from the table to get a glass of water. She didn't want David getting more upset with her. Erica checked in on Billy one last time before she and David go to bed.

Just after midnight, David woke up to empty his bladder. As he walked out of the bathroom, his attention turned towards the right into the kitchen, a series of bumps in the living room. David walked into the kitchen, turning the light on. Nothing. David waited, listened. David walked through the living room, down the hall, and pushed Billy's door open to check-in. Billy was asleep in bed. As David turned to walk away, he noticed a shadow pass against the wall.

"Erica?" David said.

He walked into the living room and back into the bedroom. Erica was asleep on her side.

Another series of bumps came from in the living room.

David sighed and whispered, "Probably the house settling. Get a grip on yourself."

4

The next morning Erica was eager to begin painting on her new easel as David left for work. As she took a sip of hot tea, she gazed out the kitchen window at the old oak tree in the backyard. The distinctive look of the oak tree inspired her to paint it on canvas. Erica has a vivid mind for painting. As a young girl living with her parents, she would go for a walk down the countryside, walking along the dusty road; to a wooden swing hanging from a huge oak branch where she would sit and free her imagination. Her mom taught her not to try too hard when casting for ideas. Her mom would say, "*The mind must be clear and unhurried when generating ideas that will catch your fancy.*"

For Erica, the longing to create something in color on canvas was what drove her to paint; an interest she picked up from her mom. Even though Erica's paintings resemble her mom's style, she searches for her own. Her quest for individuality is shown more and more as she continues to paint. To produce a good painting, she's willing to take infinite pains and do the work over again at any stage of the painting. For Erica, patience was in abundance.

Erica retrieved her new easel and painting bag from the storage room. As Erica removed the items from the bag, she began setting everything up beside the living room window, facing the oak tree in the backyard. The day was mostly cloudy which was perfect – the sun wouldn't obstruct Erica's view from getting a good initial sketch of the tree. Erica used sailcloth for her cotton canvas – satisfactory for oil paintings; paint colors made from earth pigments. Her mom never used anything else.

Erica was about halfway into her first sketch when there was a knock at the door. It was Pam.

"Hi," Pam said. "I was wondering if I could watch little Billy for you today. If you have some grocery shopping to do or…" Pam noticed the easel and paint supplies in the corner of the living room. "…anything else," Pam continued, "I can take him off your hands for a bit."

"Yes," Erica replied, "please come in."

"I won't stay long Erica. I can see you're busy." Pam stared at the Easel. "What are you painting?"

"The oak tree in the backyard. I'm just getting started."

"Well, then I won't take up more of your time. I'll get Billy and head out. We're going downtown for a few groceries. I'll buy some candy for Billy."

"Pam, wait." Erica took a deep breath before continuing. "Are you okay? After the other night?"

"What are you talking about?"

"The spirit board. I know it upset you."

Pam nodded her head lightly followed by a smile. "I'm fine Erica. Really. It's just a stupid board game. I shouldn't have let Richard drag me into such a thing."

"I was just worried about you."

"Then worry no more. I'm fine."

Erica smiled, a feeling of relief coming over her. "I'm glad Pam. Billy is in his room. He'll be glad to see you."

After Pam left with Billy, Erica stepped into her bedroom and undressed out of her pajamas. She reached for her painting clothes which consisted of a faded blue t-shirt and a pair of ragged jeans. As she began to close the closet door, she noticed the spirit board resting on the top shelf. Erica opened the closet door and stared at the old box, remembering last night. She was still curious to know what day she would die. What drove her crazy was why she wanted to know so badly. It didn't make sense to her that she was so curious. Erica knew the board wasn't real and that the answer it would give her would most likely be the wrong date. But she didn't care…she had to know.

Erica realized that her interest in painting had subsided and now she's anxious to play the board. She took the board from the closet and set it up in the living room. She didn't think she could play by herself, but she was going to try. She placed her fingers on the planchette; trying to understand how it works. She inhaled deeply, closed her eyes. "Are you with me? Here? Now?"

BANG!

Erica suddenly jumps out of her chair at the rapid knocks against the front door. Trying to catch her breath, Erica approached the door.

"Amanda," Erica said. "O my God."

"Hey sis," Amanda replied. "You look spooked."

Still breathing heavy she replied, "You might say that." Erica let Amanda come in. "What are you doing here? I figured you'd be in class today."

"It's Saturday. And I came by to see your new house! O wow sis. It's awesome!"

"Yes, it's very nice. Oh, and thanks for the new towels you sent me. We needed some new ones."

Amanda was curiously walking around, checking out the place. "This is a nice pad. I can so shack up here."

Amanda is Erica's little sister, by four years. Amanda's black hair and her taste in dark clothing would lead most folks to perceive her as worshipping the devil, yet if they were to have a short conversation with her, they would leave thinking just the opposite. Amanda is a genuinely good person with a big heart. Her dark, gothic style stems from her boyfriend Stephen Pike, who studies demonology. The subject intrigues him. Amanda resembles Erica; she's curious about the supernatural as well. And that same curiosity is what led Amanda to attend a magic show where she met Stephen.

Amanda stared at the rough sketch on the canvas. "Nice artwork sis."

"I'm just getting started."

"I remember when you used to sit on that swing down the road and doodle on your pad. I wish I had your talent."

"Desire, determination, and patience are certainly required."

"Patience is not my greatest strength. Whoa!"

Amanda's attention was drawn to the spirit board. She turned back to Erica. "Taking up a second hobby?"

"It's not a hobby," Erica replied. "It's a board game."

"Board game my tush." Amanda stood over the board, pointing at it. "It's a spirit board. You're communicating with the dead."

"The dead? C'mon. That's crazy."

"You know what's crazy? Playing this thing. It's insane."

Erica stared down at the board, not replying.

"Where did you get this? It's old."

"David found it in his dad's storage shed. He doesn't know where it came from. It was Richard's idea to give it a whirl."

Amanda laughed. "A whirl, yes. The more times you play it, the more strength it gains."

Erica shrugged her shoulders and replied, "So, what does that even mean?"

"If you mess with this thing enough, it will take over your life."

"That's ridiculous. We're talking about a board game."

Amanda stared at Erica. "Oh my God. You're hooked on it."

Erica stared back at her. "I have a strong curiosity, ok?"

"And a death wish to go with it. Gosh Erica, what are you thinking about? You need to throw this board into the trash."

"I asked a few questions when we played it; questions that no one in the room knew about me. It answered them with accuracy. I was shocked."

"And hooked."

"Yes. I can't help it."

"Stephen was telling me a story nearly a year ago. But of course, he waits 'til my soaps are on. Anyway, he tells me a story about this spirit board and then he shows me a picture of it. I didn't know what it was. I just said it looked creepy. I told him that I didn't believe that a game board could move on its own. So, being the one to prove me wrong, it did just that. He took me to a gypsy he met years earlier who had a spirit board in her workings. She invited Stephen and me to sit at the table to try it out. After several questions and answers given by the board, I stick to my defenses and claim that he moved it himself. You know what he tells me?"

"What?"

"Stephen said the board is using our subconscious minds as fuel to move to the answers. Then, he gets up and tells me to use it alone. After some hesitation, I give in. I asked a question about myself. It took more concentration, but eventually the board moved on its own. I was shocked. And the answer it gave me was correct."

Erica looked back at the board. "So, it can work with just one person."

Amanda folded the board up and placed it into the box. "I'm taking this board with me. You'll thank me later."

Erica reached for the board and snatched it from Amanda's grasp. "Stop it Amanda! This isn't your board."

"Trust me, you don't want it to be yours either sis. I'm telling you to stop messing with this thing before you get in too deep."

"That's crazy talk. I'm not in too deep."

Amanda shook her head in disappointment. "Yes, you are Erica; you just don't know it yet."

Erica didn't reply as she set the board game down on the table.

Amanda sighed. "I can't tell you what to do; even as kids you were hard-headed as concrete." She looked up at Erica. "Just don't be foolish with this board. I'm serious."

"I got it sis," Erica replied, trying to show confidence in her tone.

"I'm heading out," Amanda said, walking to the door. "I'll be back in a few days. Stephen is coming into town; perhaps we'll come by for a longer visit."

Erica smiled. "That sounds great. I'll tell David and maybe we can do some cooking on the grill and relax."

"Grill and chill. It sounds like a good time. Love you sis."

Erica closed the door as Amanda left. Erica returned to the living room, staring at her easel, then at the spirit board. "In too deep?" She pondered the thought; also, the burning question on her mind. She had to know.

Erica closed the curtains, turned off the lights, pulled a chair up to the table, unfolded the board, and placed the planchette in the center of it. Now that she knew it could move with only one player involved, there was no stopping her. She sat in silence, tuned into her breathing; concentrating as she placed her fingers on the planchette. She closed her eyes, focusing on the question that she'd been dying to ask. As she breathed in deep and slowly exhaled, the question came out.

"What is the month, day, and year that I will die."

5

Erica folded up the board, placing it back into the box. She placed the table in the corner of the room, taking the spirit board back into the bedroom closet and put it on the top shelf. She leaned on the closet door for a moment as the regret of asking the question seeped into her mind. She stared across the dark bedroom. Her eyes water up as a few tears escaped down her cheeks.

To get her mind off the board, Erica threw herself back into her painting. She still had four hours to paint before David comes home and then to pick up Billy from Pam's.

Erica focused her mind at the painting of the oak tree. She stared out the window, analyzing the tree, noticing the shape of it, the way its long, wrinkled branches reached out. Erica had sketched the tree on paper. She would end up drawing a few sketches and put them in the order in which they were done. She would select the one that interests her and work off that. Then, with a neutral color, she goes over the lines of her drawing with a brush. She doesn't bother with details at this point. Erica worked in the basic colors and schemes, then she focused on the stronger colors, in thicker pigments. Around this point, Erica stopped to evaluate her painting critically, looking for areas that seem lackluster. She would bring them to life with touches of another color. Her mom showed her how to paint for longer periods of time. For more flexibility and control over the brush, Erica would hold the brush a few inches away from the ferrule, the metal part of the brush. Her mom found that her arm would tense up less by holding the brush in this manner.

Erica was half-way into her painting when David returned home from work. Erica could tell David had a long day.

"Did you have to cover for the other guard today?" Erica asked.

"Yea," David replied. "It's starting to become a regular thing now. They need to find someone who wants to work and just let him go. He doesn't like it there anyway. He's just making it harder on the rest of us."

"Well, why don't you take a shower? I'll start cooking dinner."

"Where's Billy?" David asked.

"He's at Pam's," Erica said. "We have to pick him up."

"Do you mind going without me? I'm gonna take a shower and rest for a minute."

"Sure. Absolutely. By the way, how do you like my oil painting so far?"

David returned to the living room and stared at the painting. "It's coming together very good sweetie. I'm always amazed at how talented you are."

Erica smiled. "Thank you honey."

David walked up to Erica and kissed her passionately on her lips. "And I might add...a very sexy artist as well," David said in a soft, seductive voice.

"Keep talking like that and I may have Pam keep Billy all night."

⌐

Later that evening, after Erica returned home with Billy and David had rested for a bit, and they sat down to have dinner. Erica made her favorite Mexican casserole; she made it in an old casserole dish because she hadn't gotten around to replacing her favorite one that broke.

"So how was your day?" David asked.

"Oh, it was relaxing," Erica replied. "I got a lot of painting done, as you've seen. Amanda came by to spend time with me."

"Was she dressed like she was gonna make a pit stop at a funeral?" David asked, trying to hide his grin.

"Stop it, David," Erica replied, trying not to laugh with him. "That's my sister you're talking about. She's just different, that's all."

"She didn't start dressing like that until she met that weirdo."

"Well, although I'm inclined to agree with you, I asked her and Stephen over for an evening together."

"What will I talk to him about?" David asked.

"Anything. I'm sure he'll spill off into his theories of demons though."

"I'm betting on it."

"Perhaps he can shed some light on our new board game."

Billy sat on the opposite end of the table, listening in on their conversation.

"Seriously?" David said. "I'm not sure I'm ready to hear his version of things."

"What's the harm? It can't hurt to hear some history on it. He's majoring in the subject of demons. We may learn something interesting."

Now David knew his wife just as much as she knew herself, perhaps even more so. "Please don't tell me you and Amanda played that thing."

"On the contrary, Amanda was against playing it. She's had personal experience with one in the past. She advised us to get rid of it."

"Not a bad idea," David replied quickly. "I should return it to the shed next time we go over there."

Erica ran her fingers through her hair, hesitated, and sighed. "I asked the board when I was going to die."

David dropped his fork onto his plate. "My God," David replied, glancing over at Billy who looked down at his plate. "What has gotten into you? I told you not to ask that question. It's gonna mess with your head."

Erica shrugged, "I don't understand why you're making such a big deal out of this. It's just a game."

"Yes, that's right. It's just a game. So why don't you leave it alone."

"I'm curious. You know how I am."

"Yea I do. You can add stubborn to that list too. So, are you going to tell me what the board said or not?"

"Well, when I asked the question the first time, that moving object slid off the board. So, I asked the question again and the board said goodbye." Erica hesitated for a moment. "So, no it didn't give me an answer."

David let out a long sigh. "You talk as if that board is real. You're curious beyond reason. If Amanda was really against playing that thing, how did you convince her to play?"

"I didn't. I played it alone."

David stared at Erica for a moment, then looked over at Billy who was staring back with ears tuned in. David turned back to Erica. "I didn't think it could be played by just one person."

"Stephen told Amanda that if you concentrate hard, really focus, that one person could do it."

David shook his head. "For heaven sakes. Please tell me you'll put this to rest."

Erica stared at David for a second. "Okay, if it means that much to you, I'll stop playing it."

"Good," David replied. "Now, I say we all three cuddle up on the couch and watch some TV." David turned to

Billy. "What do you say buddy? You want to sit in the middle of mommy and daddy on the couch?"

Billy nodded his head in agreement with a huge smile.

The next morning, Richard popped in to see if David would join him in taking a walk down the trail that led into the woods. It was a favorite pastime for the brothers when they were kids. They were always adventurous with hopes they would stumble upon something worth getting into. It was David's day off and he knew that Erica would be painting for the next several hours, so he and Richard took off towards the woods. They entered the old trail that was barely visible from all the little pine trees that were growing on top of it.

Richard led the way. "Remember walking through these woods as kid's bro?"

"O yea," David replied. "All the red bugs we picked up too?"

"You think that old fort we built is still down here?"

"I doubt it. We made that thing out of plywood you know. And it wasn't the treated kind either. I'd say that fort is long gone by now. Heck, I don't remember where it was."

"It was along this trail. I know that for sure."

The brothers had walked a quarter of a mile when they came to a fork in the trail.

"Where do we go from here?" Richard asked.

"I don't know," David replied. "I don't remember this fork being here when we were kids. Let's go left for a bit and see what's down there."

The trail led the brothers downhill. As the trail turned a corner, they noticed two sheets of plywood nailed to a group of trees.

"There it is bro!" Richard said, excited. "That's our fort!"

"I don't think so Rich," David said. "This fort looks too new to be ours. But this is the place where we built our fort years ago." David looked around and noticed another trail, just barely visible, coming from the other direction. "Hey, we got on the wrong trail. Now I remember."

"What is it bro?"

David pointed east. "Look at this trail coming from that direction. Now that's our old trail. Not the one we were just on. The trail we followed must've been made years later after we grew up. That trail is ours because I remember our fort being just to the right of it."

"O yea. You're right. So, where does this trail go?"

"I don't know. I guess some kids made it years later."

Richard walked inside the fort, which was nothing more than four sheets of plywood walled in with an opening in the corner signifying a door. Richard was taking a trip down memory lane.

"Hey bro, you remember we use to bring our bb guns down here and shoot the mess out of cans and bottles?"

"O yea, I remember. I was a pretty good shooter. I don't recall you ever hitting much."

Richard rested his hands on his hips. "I always thought you bent the scope on my gun."

"Which I didn't. You were just a bad shooter."

Richard changed the subject. "How bouts we walk back to that fork and hang a right. We'll see what's down there."

The brothers made their way back to the fork. It was a more difficult walk as they were walking uphill. When they came to the fork, they rested for a minute.

"Boy," Richard said, "I remember when we could walk these trails all day long and not give out."

"Yea I know," David replied. "That was about fifteen years ago. I just don't do much walking these days. My job requires me to stand guard of a gate for eight hours a day. I do need more exercise."

The brothers turned onto the fork, heading down the opposite path. They walked down the trail, not noticing anything familiar. Just plenty of pine trees and brush. Just then, they came across an old rusted car.

"Wow," Richard said, running towards the car. "Now, I remember this car. We used to play in it when we were kids. We'd take turns driving it. We had our toy guns and we were shooting at the bad guys."

David couldn't help but laugh at the kid that still lived inside his brother. "Yea, I do remember that. It looks a lot rustier these days than I remembered."

Richard thought for a minute. "Isn't this a '40 Pontiac Sedan?"

David studied it. "That would be my guess. Not sure on the year model though."

"I'll ask daddy about this car. Maybe he knows something about it."

As David rested his hand against the rear fender, he felt an eerie vibe. David looked down into the rear window. A vision came to him…a wreck…water…a woman beating on the rear window. The feeling was intensifying as David quickly let go of the car and stepped back a few steps; his breathing heavy.

"Boy," Richard said, twisting the steering wheel, "they don't build cars like this anymore."

"We better be heading back now," David replied. "I don't want Erica thinking we got kidnapped by Bigfoot."

Richard scurried his way out of the car. "You still believe in Bigfoot bro?"

⌐

Erica placed a damp plate into the dish rack as she glanced out the kitchen window. She stared at the oak tree, trying to get a more vivid image of it. She was almost done painting the tree. All she needed was to add a few more details to it to make it come alive.

As she continued washing dishes, she began to feel uneasy – as if she was being watched. In an instant, Erica dropped her plate into the sink; it broke in half on impact. She quickly turned around, staring towards the hallway. Her heart racing. She glimpsed a shadow down the wall of the hallway.

"David is that you?" she called out.

No response. Erica slowly made her way towards the dimly lit hallway, hoping to find David just playing a trick on her, in which she would kill him afterward. The house was quiet. Erica stepped in Billy's room, then proceeded down the hallway. She peeked into the bathroom.

"David?" she called out again. No one was there. Just then, the front door swung open. Erica jumped out of her skin.

"Erica, are you okay?" David asked.

"What the hell," Erica replied. "You scared me."

"I'm sorry about that. Me and Rich just got back from the woods. Is everything okay?"

"I thought I saw someone," Erica said. "Someone walking into the hallway when I was in the kitchen."

"You think you saw someone in our house?"

"Yes. It felt so real. It was like I could feel their presence."

David began looking around. "Ok, now you're starting to scare me."

"I'm serious David. It felt like they were in this room with me."

"What about now? Do you feel the same way?"

Erica paused for a moment. "No. I don't feel it now."

"Here," David said, handing Erica a bottle of water. "Why don't you sit down for a minute and relax."

"Yea."

David opened the cabinet door above the countertop and noticed several roaches running around.

"Whoa! We got roaches in here," David said.

"Really?" Erica replied. "I've never noticed them before."

"Neither have I. Do we have some roach spray?"

"I doubt it. We used it all up at the apartment."

"Remind me to get some next time we make a trip to the market. I don't want them getting worse."

Just then, the phone rang. Erica reached for it.

"Hello," Erica said. "Yes, this is Erica Chandler. No…that's fine. I certainly can. Yes. Thank you."

"Who was that sweetie?" David asked.

"Oh my God! That was the sewing factory. I got the job! I start tomorrow morning!"

"Wow," David said. "That's great!"

Not a moment later, David and Erica couldn't help but think about the fact that the board was right about its prediction. They stared at each other for a moment.

David responded. "I'm sure it's just a coincidence."

Erica shook her head and replied with a serious tone, "I hope so."

Later that evening, David fired up the mower to cut the front lawn. Arthur Rasberry sat outside under his canopy, sipping on sweet tea. As David made a turn to head back up, he spotted the old man looking at him through the shrubs. David got to feeling a little uncomfortable; the same feeling he got from him after their first meeting. As David made his way back up towards the trailer, he drove toward the shrubs where Arthur was standing. David killed the mower, checking the tank to see if it needed more gas. What David wanted to do was strike another conversation with him.

"I'm starting to think these mowers drink more gas these days," David said.

"You and me both," Arthur replied with a crooked grin. "I keep looking underneath mine, checking for a hole."

David approached him. "How are you today?"

"I'm doing well. Just taking it one day at a time. That's what we old folks got to do these days."

David nodded. "Yes, I suppose."

"How are you and your family?"

"We're doing fine," David replied. "We've finally settled into our new home; had a housewarming party the other day. We love the location and it's very quiet here. My wife enjoys it very much and that's what matters to me."

Arthur gave the trailer his attention, studying it hard. David noticed Arthur's serious stare towards his house.

Not knowing how to respond, David cleared his throat.

Arthur responded, his eyes still fixated on the trailer. "How is it...living in that trailer of yours, Mr. Chandler?"

David hesitated for a moment. "Um...it's good. It's the first home for me and my family so there's not much to compare it to. Everything seems to be going well so far."

Arthur maintained eye contact with the trailer until David finished, then the old man slowly turned his gaze toward David. "So far…huh?"

"If you don't mind me asking sir, why do you have so much concern for my family regarding our home?"

Arthur didn't respond as he returned glances at the trailer.

David continued. "Is there something I should know about?"

"You're concerned," Arthur replied. "You tell me."

"Our home seems to have your full attention. You tell me."

The old man narrowed his eyes. "I believe there's something strange about that trailer Mr. Chandler."

"What are you talking about?"

"I think you would agree with me."

"Why would I agree with you?"

Arthur didn't respond. He continued his stare at David as if he knew something about him that David didn't want to share.

David shoved his hands in his pockets and replied, "If you have something to say, now is the time."

Arthur shuffled his feet and smiled, "When you want to have a serious conversation about this, then let me know." Arthur turned and slowly began walking away.

"Talk about what?" David shouted.

David watched as Arthur continued at a slow pace to his front door, never looking back. David sighed, and in a moment of frustration, he pulled out a small rock and threw it towards the woods across the road. *Could the old man know something about that trailer? Something that could put them in danger?*

As David fired up the mower, he turned around to look at the trailer, staring for a few seconds. An unsettling feeling came over him; much like the feeling he felt when he placed his hand on that rusty Pontiac Sedan.

6

The next morning, Erica got Billy ready to drive over to Pam's. Erica was excited, yet nervous about her first day on her new job. David had already left for work.

Arthur Rasberry noticed that everyone was leaving. His curiosity was getting the best of him. He wanted to go inside the trailer; look around and get a feel of the place. He wanted to get close to the trailer to understand why he felt so strange about it. There was something in or around the trailer that was drawing him to it; a kind of energy that was luring him there. He couldn't tell whether the energy was negative or positive. He had to know what it is that's bugging him.

Two hours had passed since Erica left to drop off Billy. Arthur stepped through the shrubs, over onto the Chandler's lot. It had been years since he'd step foot on this little piece of property. As the old man slowly made his way to the trailer, he began running through his memory of the times that he and his family spent together. Good times.

But as he eyed the trailer, getting closer to it, the memories began to fade away and the feeling of fear came over him. He stood about twenty feet from the trailer, looking at it from left to right. The trailer was faded white with a pale green trim that ran along the top of the trailer from one end to the other. Rust lines trailed from the rooftop, made from calcium and lime buildup.

Arthur could see the blocks holding the trailer up. The Chandler's hadn't placed skirting around it yet. The trailer looked normal, yet he couldn't shake the feeling he had brewing inside of him. He began walking towards the small deck that David built around the back door. As he walked up the steps, he thought he heard something inside. He paused, listening closely. All he could hear were the sounds of cars passing by on the highway in the distance. He inched closer to the back door. It was locked. Arthur made his way around the other side of the trailer, looking at the windows that were covered with the new curtains that Erica bought. He walked up the small steps to the front door that was locked. Suddenly, the old man had a strange feeling come over him. He began to feel sick suddenly. Arthur stepped back from the trailer, holding his stomach. It felt like knives being shoved into his abdomen. He bent forward in pain, holding his stomach. He started walking away from the trailer and the pain slowly began to fade away.

Arthur wiped the sweat from his forehead as he took another glance at the trailer before making his way through the shrubs. He noticed the curtains move in the north room of the trailer…David and Erica's bedroom. At first, he thought it could be a fan blowing, but then he noticed a shadow pass across the window. Arthur stood in shock; his knees knocking so loud he could almost hear them. His heart was beating rapidly as he could only think there was someone or something inside the trailer. Arthur ran towards his house as fast as his wiry legs could take him. Not since his track and field days had he ever moved so fast. At that point, he wasn't worried about fracturing bones or pulling a muscle. He had to get inside his house and call the police.

In minutes, a patrol car pulled into the Chandler's driveway. A police officer stepped out of the car, with her hand on her gun holster. From Arthur's panicked voice, stating that someone was inside his neighbor's home, the officer approached the house cautiously. Arthur was peeking through the shrubs as the officer made her way towards the trailer. After making a trip around the trailer, the officer came over to Arthur. She wanted a statement about what he saw. Arthur didn't mention that he was snooping around the place.

Pam was driving past the trailer when she noticed the police car in the driveway.

"Hold on Billy," Pam said, as she turned around and drove in.

Pam introduced herself to the officer. Billy was standing next to her.

"Do you have a spare key to the home?" the officer asked Pam.

"Yes," Pam replied. "I'll let you in."

Erica had given Pam a spare key just in case she needed some things from Billy's room. The officer entered the trailer; looking around for anything that was out of the ordinary. There was no sign of a break-in. Everything was normal. The officer entered David and Erica's bedroom. She stared at the curtain that was covering the window.

Before the officer left, she informed Arthur that she saw no sign of a break-in and everything was ok. Arthur still couldn't shake the feeling he had about the trailer. Whoever or whatever was in the trailer was gone by the time the officer got there.

⌒

When David returned home that evening, he went to make a sandwich. As he picked up the loaf of bread, he noticed small holes in it.

"Jesus Christ," David said. "Roaches."

David tossed the loaf into the trash can. He settled on a bowl of cereal instead after careful inspection of the box.

About thirty minutes later, Erica arrived. Together, they went over to Richard and Pam's to get Billy.

~

"He did what?" David shouted.

"Yes," Pam said. "He thought he saw someone in your house, so he called the police to check it out. The officer asked me to let her in to investigate, but everything checked out ok."

"You damn right everything is ok," David said. "Everything but our nosey neighbor. He has been on us ever since we moved here."

Erica turned to David. "What do you mean?"

"He's been curious about our house. He says there's something not right about it. When I asked him to explain, he refused to tell me."

"He thought he saw someone in your bedroom," Pam said. "Like a shadow passing across the window is how he explained it to the officer."

Erica looked at David frightened. "What if he's right?"

"Sweetie, the man has gone senile. He's got nothing better to do than to mess with us about this. He probably doesn't like us living there for some reason. It could be that he's used to his privacy. Before we moved in, he didn't have neighbors and he lived alone. He's just trying to scare us away."

"It doesn't make any sense though," Erica said.

David shook his head in disgust. "Look, let's just take Billy and go home," David said. "I've had a hard day at work and I'm ready to just relax for the rest of the evening."

"Well," Pam said, "if you two want a quiet evening together, I can keep Billy overnight. I don't mind it at all. Richard is working late tonight."

Erica stepped over to Pam, showing concern. "I'd rather take Billy home tonight Pam. Maybe tomorrow night will be better."

Pam nodded her head. "Of course, Erica."

"I just thought you need a break," Erica replied.

"Oh gosh no," Pam said. "Billy's no trouble at all. I love spending time with him. I really do."

David and Erica looked at Pam, then swapped glances at each other.

"Well, we'll be going now," David said. "Goodbye Pam. Tell Richard I'll see him later."

Pam watched as they backed out of the driveway and headed down the road.

David looked over at Billy, then at Erica. "Do you think Pam is okay?"

"I was just thinking the same thing," Erica replied.

⁓

1:00 AM

David and Erica awoke to the sound of a door slam on the other side of the trailer.

Erica turned to David in the darkroom, whispering, "Did you hear that?"

"Yea," David replied. "Do you think it was Billy?"

Erica pulled away the covers. "I'm going to check on him."

David rose from the bed to turn on the lamp. Erica was already out of bed when the lights came on and there was Billy, standing next to the bed on David's side.

"Oh my God!" David shouted, sliding over to Erica's side. "You scared me Billy!"

"Billy, are you okay?" Erica asked.

"I saw a man standing in the door," Billy said.

David jumped out of bed. "Both of you stay here."

Erica covered her mouth. "My God, maybe Mr. Rasberry was right."

David walked out of the bedroom and turned on the lights in the kitchen. The first thing he noticed was all the tiny roaches on the countertop. "Jesus!" He began stomping on the bigger ones running across the floor as he made his way towards the hallway. He couldn't help but think about what Mr. Rasberry claimed to have seen. *A shadow passing across the window. Could this man be that shadow?*

David couldn't think straight. He was nervous. Scared. He had chill bumps on his arms again. He checked the front door. It was still locked. He glanced into Billy's room. Nothing.

"Billy," Erica said as she kneeled to her son, "what exactly did you see?"

"A man," Billy calmly replied, "standing in the door."

"What door are you talking about?"

"My door."

David checked the back door. It was locked as well. He stood silent, listening for sounds. He peeked in the spare bedroom; nothing was out of place.

Erica cupped Billy's face in her arms. "What was the man doing?"

Billy shrugged. "He was just looking at me."

"What did he look like?"

Billy thought for a moment. "An army man…with a gun."

Suddenly, David felt as if someone was watching him from behind; the feeling of someone's presence overwhelmed him. He didn't want to turn around; afraid of what he might see. He could feel it watching him, a powerful presence. David quickly turned around. No one was there. David could smell a distinct odor in the air. It smelled like an old antique store; the one from the spirit board; the same smell from that old antique store in New Orleans years ago. "What the hell is going on?"

"Billy," Erica said, "did you have a dream?"

"No mommy," Billy replied. "It wasn't a dream. It was real."

Erica could tell that Billy was frightened; the look on his face expressing the need for comfort and safety assurance from his mom. Erica gave him a huge hug. "Don't worry baby. Everything's gonna be okay."

"Who was that man mommy?" Billy asked.

"I don't know sweetie," Erica said, not knowing how to explain ghosts to Billy. "Daddy will find out who it is, ok?"

David returned to the bedroom.

Erica stood up. "Well, did you find anything?"

David sighed. "Nothing."

7

Erica's thoughts muddled over the possibility that she and David could have a ghost living with them as she made breakfast for Billy the next morning.

Erica wasn't focused on going to work. Her thoughts were on Arthur and what he saw through their bedroom window and the incident that happened the night before. If a ghost was haunting their trailer, then it had to be from the spirit board. She began thinking about the question she asked. *What day will I die?* She gravely regretted the decision.

Erica walked over to the sink to wash down a plate, just to make sure it was clean of roach deposits. As she dried the plate off, she looked out towards the oak tree and noticed someone standing beside it. The glass in the window was old and foggy; it wasn't clear enough for her to determine who it was. Erica walked over to the large window in the living room to get a better view. She was shocked as she stared at the silhouette of a woman and child standing next to the oak tree. Erica couldn't stop staring at them. The woman was dressed in all white and the child was a little girl, about seven years old and wearing a white dress with red polka dots. The little girl was holding a teddy bear in her left hand and clutching the woman's white dress with her right hand. The woman looked too old to be the girl's mother – perhaps her grandmother. They looked so real as they stood near the tree. The little girl looked up at the mother, then looked towards the trailer. Erica could see the features of their faces. Erica could still see the oak tree through their transparent bodies. They were content; peaceful. It looked as though they were spending time together, enjoying the day. Erica walked over to the back door, opened it, and looked out towards the oak tree. In that split second, they were gone. Erica had no doubt that she was looking at ghosts. A tear ran down her cheek as she continued staring at the oak tree. She felt a connection with them. But why?

Later that day, Arthur was hard at work, planting flowers around his house. This time every year, Arthur and his late wife would plant tulips in the corner of the house, adjacent to the front door. He would glance towards the trailer next door, remembering what happened just the other day.

Deciding to stretch his legs, Arthur made his way over to the shrubs to take a closer look. He noticed that the Chandler's were gone. He glanced over to the bedroom window where he saw the shadow. He noticed the curtains moving slightly. Maybe this time it was a fan blowing. Then he thought he saw the shadow again. His first instinct was to call the police, but he decided against it. If the police came over again and found nothing, they may cart him to the nuthouse.

David came home that afternoon after picking up Billy. He settled in with a nice hot bath like always. Afterward, he sat down to watch TV as Erica came home.

"So how was your day honey?" David asked.

"Stressful, but good," Erica replied. "I think I'll like it better once I get used to how things run. I'm still a green thumb."

"I have some news to tell," David said.

"Please share," Erica replied.

"I'm being transferred to overnight."

"Wow, you'll be working nights now?"

"Yep, just like the old days. I think it will be better for me. Not to mention a change of pace."

"Well that's great. I don't guess it'll pose a problem for Billy."

"I don't think so. We can let Pam keep him more often. I mean, she seems to want to anyway."

Erica thought about that for a moment. "Yea…"

"I had a talk with Pam about it today when I picked up Billy."

"What did she say?"

"She was excited about it. She said she'd love to."

Erica looked away. "I don't doubt that."

ᕓ

That evening, Erica joined David in the living room with two glasses of sweet tea and they snuggled on the couch. She lit a candle sitting on the end table David picked up from the junk shed.

"I've been thinking," Erica said.

"About what?" David asked.

"Let's say we do have ghosts living in our trailer. How do we know if they're evil?"

David thought for a second. "Well, we don't. They haven't done anything to harm us…yet."

"I'm thinking that the ghosts are good-natured."

"You do?"

Erica took a sip of tea. "This morning I saw a transparent image of a woman and child, standing near the oak tree in the backyard. They looked peaceful, content; harmless."

David leaned up. "Wait a minute," David said, putting his glass of tea down on the end table. "You actually saw a ghost...in the daytime?"

"Yes, I did. They looked so real. But they also looked innocent."

"You could tell what they looked like?"

"Yes, very much so. If I could see them again, I'd want to paint them into my oil painting of the oak tree. I've got a clear, vivid image of them already. I wish you could see them."

David looked away. "Yeah. Me too."

"So, I'm thinking that our ghosts are not evil. They're not demons or evil spirits, but more like angels."

A quizzical look appeared on David's face. "Angels? You think so?"

"If you could see what I saw this morning, you would think the same thing. I felt a connection to them; it was a feeling of serenity."

David shook his head. "That's not how I'd explain what I felt that night Billy was standing next to our bed."

Erica tilted her head. "What are you talking about?"

"Erica, I felt a presence behind me in the hallway; a terrifying presence."

Erica didn't reply.

"I can't explain it, but it sure didn't feel good."

∾

After putting Billy to bed, Erica made her way into the bedroom. David was already lying in bed with the light on, reading a car magazine.

Erica crawled into bed with a seductive look on her face, hoping David would notice. But he didn't. He was so buried into that car magazine he wouldn't have noticed if she was wearing a sexy lace lingerie.

Erica slid under the covers. "Do you realize that we're not going to be sleeping together much anymore," she said.

"I know," David replied, disappointment in his tone. "But there's not much I can do about it. The boss didn't leave me any choice."

Erica slid her finger across David's chest. "So why don't we make the best of it, while we've still got the chance."

David closed the magazine and turned to Erica with a seductive smile of his own.

Erica crawled over and positioned herself over David, holding him down. She snatched the magazine from him and threw it on the floor. Erica leaned over and began kissing him. With a giggle, Erica reached up and turned the lamp off.

2:38 AM

Erica woke up startled, hearing a constant creaking sound coming from the living room. She turned towards David who was still asleep. The sound continued. Erica nudged David in his left rib.

"Honey, wake up," Erica whispered.

"Huh? What is it?" David whispered.

"You hear that?"

David listened for a few seconds. "It sounds like our rocking chair."

"That's what I thought. It's rocking back and forth."

"Do you think it's Billy?"

"I don't think so. Billy wouldn't do that."

"Let's sneak in there slowly and find out what's going on," David said as he and Erica slowly crept out of bed.

They pushed the bedroom door open. The sound of the chair was very clear now. They tiptoed through the darkness, into the kitchen. A streetlight cast through the windows, enough for David and Erica to notice what looked like dozens of little roaches scurrying on the countertops and along the baseboards.

They could see the back of the rocking chair in the living room. It was still rocking. The chair was facing the hallway. David slowly made his way towards it as Erica stayed behind. He wanted to peek around the chair to see if anyone was in it. By now, David's heart was beating in his throat. His breathing was heavy. The nervous pit deep in his stomach was enough to bring him to his knees. When David was about four feet away from the chair, it stopped…instantly. David peeked around the chair to see that no one was in it. He turned to Erica who was in shock. David reached and turned the kitchen lights on to notice way too many roaches not to call it an infestation. Suddenly, David and Erica were killing off roaches until there were none left to see.

"Damn roaches," David said quietly. "Where are they coming from?"

"I don't know," Erica said. "David, there's no way that chair could've moved like that on its own."

"I know," David replied, looking around. "And I have that unsettling feeling again."

8

David and Erica didn't get much sleep that night. Erica had to go to work and David watched over Billy 'til 1:00 that afternoon before heading to work. Around that time, David took Billy over to Richard and Pam's.

"Hey bro," Richard said, walking out onto the front porch. "You look like you could use some rest."

Pam walked out and took Billy from David. "There's my little one," Pam said to Billy. "You're in for a treat; I'm taking you to town to get us some slow-churned ice cream."

Richard shook his head at Pam. "You need to take me down to get some ice cream."

Pam looked up at Richard with a smile. "You can come along. I can handle two babies."

David chuckled. "You sure about that?"

Richard smirked at David's remark. "Funny man, huh?"

"Don't worry about Billy," Pam said. "He's in good hands."

"Thanks Pam," David replied. "Erica and I sure appreciate it."

"You want something to drink?" Pam asked David.

"I'll have what Rich is having," David said, pointing to the Mountain Dew his brother was holding.

David sat down in one of the plastic chairs on the porch. Richard sat down next to him. "You and Erica must've had a long night. Ya'll working on the nightshifts, huh." Richard winked at David.

David smiled, knowing what his brother was thinking. "Erica and I have been dealing with some things lately."

Richard looked down, serious expression coming over him. "Oh, Bro. I didn't know you and Erica were having trouble in your marriage."

"Oh, no. Everything is okay in our relationship. No, it's about that spirit board. I think something came through when we were playing it that first time."

Richard leaned forward, spewing up a mouthful of soda. "Are you serious?"

"I'm afraid so. As silly as it sounds, I think our house is haunted."

Pam had retrieved David's drink but hesitated to go outside. She was on the other side of the door, listening to the conversation they were having. It was easy to hear them. The trailer was much like David and Erica's. With no insulation, sounds from outside could easily be heard from inside. Pam turned to glance at Billy, who was on the floor playing with some army men and tankers. Her concern, no doubt, was about Billy living in that house. She was concerned about his safety. She listened in closely. Her ear pressed up against the wall.

"You know," Richard said, "I've heard about things happening to people who play the spirit board, but I never believed it. There was this story about three kids just out of high school. They got the idea to drive down to that old cemetery in Vernon to solve the mystery of the ghost light, said to circle the cemetery at the stroke of midnight. So, the three of them drive down there and turning off onto that small dirt road that leads into the woods. That cemetery is located about two miles down into the thicket of that wooded area. When they reach the old rusty gates of the cemetery, they park there and set up for a séance. They gather in a circle in the bed of the truck and open the spirit board, balancing it on their knees. They try to concentrate, but with the eerie look of the cemetery in the foreground, it was difficult to do anything but sit still, trying not to breathe too loud."

David listened with skepticism as Richard continued. "It was the dead of winter, but it seemed much colder to the three boys as they sat in the back of the truck, waiting for the light to show itself. It was ten minutes 'til midnight when they heard something in the distance; the sound of an animal moving slowly towards the cemetery. One of the teenagers asks the board a question. "Are you with us?" The board said *yes*. Then, the boy next to him grabbed his own throat, like he was choking on something. He fell out of the truck. The other two rushed to his aid, but it was too late. A spirit had possessed him. He came up off the ground, grabbing one of the boys by the head, trying to kill him. The other boy was trying his best to release his grip, but he couldn't. As the demon continued holding his grip on the other boy's head, the older boy reached in the truck for holy water and doused it on him. The demon began to smoke. He released his grip and both boys fell to the ground. At the hospital, the boy who was possessed said he didn't remember anything after hearing the sound in the cemetery."

"Oh, come on," David said, shaking his head. "Did that happen? Or is this another one of your wild stories."

"That really happened," Richard replied. "The guy I work with told me. The boy that was possessed is his nephew."

"That's horrible. What if that ends up happening to me or Erica, or worse, Billy?"

Pam's heart skipped a beat. Her worries for Billy had escalated to new heights.

"Come on bro," Richard said. "It could happen to me or Pam too. Remember, you two weren't the only ones who played the board that night."

"Yea, but I think the hauntings occur where the board was played. And besides, Erica and I played it again the next night."

"Are you kidding? I thought you hated it?"

"Erica scared me with one question she was just so curious to ask. She wanted to know when she was going to die."

Richard almost came up with another mouthful of soda. "Why?"

"Don't ask me. I don't know what she was thinking." But she ended up playing the board one more time, alone. She asked the same question, but the board never gave her an answer. Thank God."

"Are you telling me a person can play alone and get a response?"

"That's what Amanda told Erica. You know, Amanda has that weirdo boyfriend of hers; Stephen Pike."

"Trust me. No one wants to know when they're gonna die. If the board told her she would die next week, she would go crazy, doing things like sky diving or rock climbing. You know, stuff people do when they've only got a few days to live."

David was in serious thought as he stared away.

"Hey bro, you still with me?"

"Something tells me I should get rid of that board. I told myself next time I come here I would put that board right back in the shed where we found it. What's to stop Erica from finding out when she's gonna die when I'm at work or something? And she can keep the answer to herself."

"If she mentions going kayaking down a level five river, you'll know," Richard said, chuckling.

"What I ought to do is bring that spirit board down here and stick it in your closet."

"Yea, and if something pops out, you'll hear me scream from two miles away."

David bursts out in laughter. "Yea, I bet so."

"Oh," Richard said, "speaking of the spirit board, I found out that Mr. Rasberry owned it."

David turned slowly turned to Richard, then stood from his seat; his expression turning ghostly. "Who told you that?"

"Dad," Richard replied. "He said Mr. Rasberry bought the board in a garage sale for 25 cents and two weeks later, it predicted the death of his wife."

David stared out into the clear vacant lot next to Richard's place.

Richard continued. "The spirit board said that Mr. Rasberry's wife would die in a car accident. When he asked the board what kind of car, the board said it was the '40 Pontiac that he drove; the very same car we found in those woods the other day. After that, he gave the board to dad because dad was curious about it himself."

"I can't believe it."

"Here's the clincher. His wife ended up dying in that very same car. The board was right all along."

David turned to Richard. "So, why did Arthur place the car down in those woods?"

"Because that used to be their backyard. He and his wife lived there before she died. After her death, he pushed the car further into the woods to where it sits now. Mr. Rasberry moved across the street. The old house stayed there until new owners bought the land. The house was unlivable, so they tore it down. That's why we didn't know about the house as kids. It was already gone by then. That explains why dad would tell us to be careful not to step on any tacks. Remember?"

David stood there quietly, trying to digest everything. "I thought I hated that board before, but now I despise it. How can that board make such a prediction like that and it holds true? And the events happened exactly how it was predicted."

"I don't know, but you better not bring that board around me ever again."

David stared at his brother in awe. He pointed towards the junk shed before making his point. "You're the one who wanted to play the damn thing, so don't be telling me what to do with it."

Richard took a sip of his drink. "What are you gonna do with it bro?"

David shook his head. "I don't know. One thing's for sure. I'm not gonna play it ever again. And neither is Erica."

Pam had heard enough. If the board was able to make predictions with such accuracy, then it had to be right about the fact that she'll never get pregnant. Pam figured if she would just face it and accept the truth, then she could move on. She stared down at Billy, worried that he may be in danger. She couldn't let anything happen to him. She had to protect him.

Pam walked out with David's soda. "Here you are David," Pam said.

"Oh, thanks Pam," David replied, popping the top.

Pam turned to Richard. "I'm going back in to get ready for town."

David stares at the junk shed. "It's interesting that dad told you all that."

"Yeah," Richard replied, "it is."

David took another sip of soda. "It makes me wonder."

"About what?"

"Mr. Rasberry gave the board to dad. What was dad so curious about?"

9

That evening, Erica dropped by the house to take a shower before picking up Billy from Pam's. Erica stood underneath the hot shower, trying to relax from a long day on the job. Various thoughts popped in her head. *Will Pam be okay as a babysitter for Billy, or is she getting too attached? Who were the woman and child standing next to the oak tree? Will I ever get that damn painting done? I never thought I'd live in a haunted house. Is the board right about my death?*

As Erica was drying off, she glanced at the fogged mirror above the vanity and noticed three small letters in the bottom right corner. She thought her mind was playing tricks on her as she walked up to the mirror for a closer look. The letters were small but much defined. They weren't in line to make a word, but they were there. Put together, the letters spelled '*out*'. She quickly took her towel and rubbed the mirror down, erasing the letters.

Erica was a little distraught as she walked up to Pam's front door. Pam was inside watching TV and Billy was playing with toys in the other room.

"Oh Pam," Erica said, "I can't stay long. I've got a lot of work to do at home."

"That's fine Erica," Pam said. "I'm just sitting here thinking to myself."

Erica turned her attention to the TV. "I didn't know you watched courtroom drama?"

"Oh," Pam said, reaching for the remote, "I wasn't aware of what was on." She turned the station.

"Are you okay?" Erica asked, with a concerned look.

"Not really. I've been thinking a lot about Richard and me." She looked up at Erica. "I don't think I'll ever get pregnant."

Erica sat down on the couch next to Pam, knowing that this would take a few minutes. "Look Pam. You're worried about this too much. The stress you're putting into this is probably the reason why you haven't become pregnant yet. You and Richard should slow down and just take it one day at a time. Don't try to put too much emphasis on it."

"But that's what we've been doing for the last year," Pam said, raising her voice. "Taking it slow. One day at a time. And look at where it's got us."

"Sometimes it takes couples longer to have a baby than it does others. You need to give it time. That's all I'm saying."

"I appreciate your concern, but I think the board is right. I'll never become pregnant...ever."

Erica's eyes widened. "Don't listen to that board. Don't give it power over you. If you think you won't ever get pregnant, then that's exactly what will happen. You've got to think positive."

"But I have been positive Erica. For the last year that me and Richard have been together I've been positive. But the board's predictions were right. It answered everyone's questions correctly."

Erica didn't respond.

"It even told your neighbor Mr. Rasberry that his wife was going to die in a car accident and that's exactly what happened. So maybe it was right about me."

Erica quickly turned to Pam. "Wait! Who told you that?"

Pam looked away for a moment. "I overheard Richard tell David that Arthur Rasberry had the board before he gave it to their father."

"Mr. Rasberry's wife died in a car wreck just like the board predicted?"

Pam nodded.

"Look Pam," Erica said, "you can't believe what that board tells you. It's just a game."

"It's just a game. It's just a game. Well, if it's just a game, then how did it know the answers to the questions we asked it? How do you explain that?"

Erica sat there for a moment. "I can't. Maybe it was a…"

"Coincidence?" Pam said, cutting Erica off. "Was that what you were about to say? We are officially beyond coincidences here. That board knew those answers. It knows that I'll never get pregnant. There was a spirit beyond the darkness who knows everything, and we made contact with it that night. It said I wasn't going to get pregnant, so that's that."

"If my memory serves me correctly, it slid off the board when you asked the question. That doesn't necessarily mean that you won't get pregnant."

Pam looked down, picking lint off her shirt.

"Look," Erica said, "there are other options for having a child. You and Richard could adopt."

"No! Pam shouted. "That's what my sister said the other day. I'm not adopting. It's out of the question."

"I'm sorry Pam. I didn't mean to upset you. I'm just trying to let you know that there are other ways of having a child."

"You see little Billy?"

Erica turned her attention to the other room where Billy was playing. She couldn't see him, but she could hear him in there.

"Little Billy may be the only child I'll ever have," Pam said with tears in her eyes. "And soon he'll be older, and you won't need a babysitter to care for him."

Erica was startled. She didn't understand exactly what Pam was saying, but she knew it wasn't good. "I'm sorry Pam. Just please don't worry about this. It will all work out. I just know it will."

ᒷ

3:12 AM

Erica woke up, hearing Billy crying. She got out of bed and walked into the kitchen, turning the light on. Roaches began scattering for cover; the infestation continued even though she and David had sprayed all over the place. As Erica approached the hallway, the crying stopped abruptly. Erica opened Billy's bedroom door and noticed that Billy was asleep.

"Billy?" Erica whispers. "You okay?"

Billy didn't respond. Erica stepped next to his bed. She placed her hand on his forehead, then pulls the covers up to his neck. She glanced over at his nightlight before stepping towards the bedroom door. As she begins to pull the door to, the nightlight begins to flicker. Erica peeked into the room, staring at the nightlight that eventually stops. Erica questioned whether she heard Billy crying as she walked back to her bedroom, killing a few roaches in her path.

4:56 AM

Erica woke up again to the sound of a baby crying. She sat up in bed on her back, staring at the ceiling, listening to the cries. *"That's not Billy crying."* She could tell it was a boy crying though. The cry was coming from the other side of the trailer. Unable to stand it any longer, Erica jumped out of bed and headed toward Billy's room. By the time she reached the living room, the crying faded away. Erica checked in on Billy who is still asleep. Nightlight still on. Erica headed back to her bedroom to try and get two more hours of sleep.

ᶜ

Morning arrived as David returned home from work. Erica was up, making breakfast and getting ready for work.

With weary eyes, David smiled at Erica and kissed her. "Did everything go ok last night?" David asked.

Erica turned to David, with droopy eyes. "Not too good," she replied.

"Why? What happened?"

"Well, for starters, we may need to rethink Pam as a babysitter."

"What do you mean? I thought Pam was doing a good job at keeping Billy."

"Well, she is, but her desperation to have a child is affecting her emotionally. And she's thinking that Billy may be the only child she'll ever spend time with. She told me that."

"I think you're looking into this way too much. Richard and Pam have been trying to have a child for a year now, but I don't see what that has to do with babysitting Billy."

"Well, in a mother's eyes, Billy is like the child that Pam will never have. That's how she sees it…I think."

"You don't seem too sure about it."

"Well, I'm not certain. Pam told me last night that Billy may be the only child she'll ever have. That stuck with me.

And she believes the spirit board when it predicted she wouldn't get pregnant."

"O come on. Richard told me that Pam is very emotional at times. I think this is one of those times. I say we overlook it for now because Pam is the only babysitter we have."

"Yea, perhaps. However, I think we should contemplate the alternative if things get worse."

David swallowed a glass of water. "Of course. Now, what else happened?"

Erica ran her fingers through her hair. "I thought I heard Billy crying last night. So, I went to check on him and he was asleep."

"You mean, he wasn't crying when you got to his room?"

"Right. I was hearing a baby cry. That's what woke me up. It sounded distant like it was coming from the other side of the trailer. I heard it again later in the night. As I listened to it, it didn't sound like Billy. You know, the way he cries."

"Ghosts?"

"My thoughts exactly."

"I'm getting rid of that board, by the way," David said, walking into the kitchen. He noticed a few roaches on the countertops. "And why are these roaches still hanging around? I've emptied three cans of roach spray on 'em."

Erica wiped the countertop with a dish rag. "And I keep the whole kitchen clean, so there's nothing for them to eat. Maybe we should call an exterminator."

"That's a good idea. I'll give one a call this morning. But I need a shower and some food."

"And I need to go to work. You want me to take Billy over to Pam's then?"

David looked at Erica with concern. "Yeah, just until we can find another babysitter. You know we'll have to pay for a babysitter. Pam does it for nothing. But like I said, Pam was just probably going through an emotional phase. I'm sure there's nothing to worry about."

Erica turned to David. "I hope you're right."

～

After Erica left with Billy, David jumped in the shower. Just after turning the water off, he heard the front door shut loudly. "Erica is that you?" he called out. No response. David waited a second. Then he heard another sound that he couldn't explain. David wrapped the towel around himself and walked out into the hallway, dripping water. The front door was locked. David made his way down the hall, into the living room. He figured if Erica was here, then she would be late for work. It was ten minutes past eight. He looked over to the front door. It was unlocked and the chain was off. He remembered locking it up just after Erica left. He quickly assumed someone was in the house.

He stepped into the kitchen. Everything seemed fine. From behind, the bathroom door slammed shut! David turned around so fast he didn't remember making the move. His heart was beating like thunder against his chest. He was gasping for every breath he took. He made his way to the bathroom and opened the door. To his surprise, the shower was turned back on. Scalding hot water was flowing from the showerhead and the whole room was becoming foggy. David walked over to the faucet and turned it off, feeling the sting of the hot water bounce on his arm. David turned towards the foggy mirror to read the letters *o u t.*

David moved in closer. "Out?" David shouted. He took the towel wrapped around his waist and with one stroke, wiped the letters away from the mirror. Frustrated, David stormed out of the bathroom, butt naked, heading down the hallway and into his bedroom. He opened the closet door and snatched the spirit board from the top shelf. With the spirit board firmly in his hands, David walked back into the living room and opened the back door. "It's you who's out!" David shouted as he threw the spirit board into the backyard.

10

Erica was touching up her painting of the oak tree the following morning as David was asleep. It was Saturday and Erica had been itching to paint the image she saw days prior.

As Erica took another look out the window at the oak tree, she focused hard on what she saw. The woman and child, standing next to the tree. Erica looked down to grab a thin brush. As she raised back up, Erica's eyes widened. The elder woman and young child stood in the same spot next to the oak tree. Erica gazed at them, barely moving; the woman tilting her head down to look at the girl. The girl raised her head to meet the woman's eyes. She was swaying her teddy bear back and forth in her left hand; the bear seemed to be soaked as drops of water fell from it. Erica focused hard at them, observing every detail, trying to get a vivid, mental picture of them that will remain in her memory.

Erica's mom had touched basis on portrait painting with her. Her mom once said that *"the portrait you paint can only record what you've seen. Seeing is even more important than understanding color or knowing how to handle the brush."* Erica has practiced portrait painting by studying photographs from magazines. She never dreamed of painting an image of ghosts.

Then, right before her eyes, the woman and the little girl vanished. Erica had not only concluded that she had seen a real ghost, but she now had a clear picture of what they look like. Without hesitation, Erica began painting as fast as she could, while the memory of the ghosts was still fresh in her mind. She cleared her head of everything that had happened to her, David, and Billy and put her complete focus into that canvas. She was determined as ever to replicate her vision…her vision of her first real ghost sighting.

⌐

That afternoon, David awoke from his nap. He had forgotten what it was like to work the graveyard shift. He remembered not getting much sleep. More like day naps were all he could muster up.

It was around four when David walked into the living room to see Erica still hard at work on her painting. Usually, about this time of the day, he'd smell something delicious cooking on the stove when Erica was off. Not today. She hadn't noticed what time it was. David smiled as he watched his wife work diligently on her art.

"You're determined to get that done I see," David said.

"Oh," Erica replied, turning around quickly, "I didn't hear you wake up."

"I thought you were about done with that piece."

"I am now," Erica said, putting the final touches on the painting. She smiled back at David. "You're in for a treat."

David clapped his hands together. "Alright. Let's see it."

"Before I show it to you, there's something I need to tell you."

David became worried. "It doesn't sound good."

"Well, I don't know. It all depends on how you take it. I saw the woman and child again this morning."

"Really? Again?"

"Yes. And this time, they stayed longer; enough time for me to get a good visual on them and paint them into my canvas."

Erica grabbed the easel and swung it around to face David.

"This is what they look like," Erica said.

David stepped closer to look at the painting. "This is a very beautiful painting Erica. The colors are so deep and natural." David looked at Erica. "I didn't know you could paint so well."

Erica smiled. "It's amazing how we're still finding out new things about each other, huh?"

David turned his attention back to the painting. "So, these are the ghosts you saw?"

"Yes. What do you think?"

"They're so real. So beautiful. But who are they?"

"I don't know, but I sure would like to find out."

"They can't be the ghosts that have been giving us problems around here."

"I've seen them twice. They don't look like the kind of ghosts that would cause problems. They seem friendly. It's like they're enjoying just spending time with each other."

David and Erica stared at the painting as it slowly dried. Minutes later, there was a knock at the door. "That's got to be the exterminator," David said.

"Thank God," Erica cried out. "Roach relief!"

A heavy man made his way into the house, looking at corners and ceilings. "Well I heard yawls got a roach problem, huh?"

"Something like that," David said, thinking about the ghosts as well.

"My name is Greg. I'll be your roach exterminator. You're my last stop for the day, thank the Lord. It's been steady since eight this morning."

David shoved his hands in his pockets. "We'd appreciate your work on getting these roaches out of here."

"This process won't take much of your time. What I'll do is look over the house and determine the severity of your problem. Then I'll scout the perimeter of the house, looking underneath. I may even take a sample of your soil if I find it necessary. The process will take about thirty minutes to an hour to complete. The sun will be setting about that time anyway. How does that sound to ya?"

"Hey," Erica said, "if it kills the roaches, then that sounds good to me."

"Okay," Greg said, sitting down on the couch. "First let's get the paperwork out of the way. All is required is both your John Hancock's on this here contract."

David and Erica quickly signed their names on the contract.

"Okay, easy enough," Greg said, putting the contract away. "Here is some reading material about the services we provide. So if you get bored, now you have something to read. Oh, and if you ever need our services again, call this number. Hopefully, it will be just for a checkup."

"Thanks," David said, a little doubt seeping from his voice. He didn't do any research or compare different companies for exterminating roaches. He just grabbed the phone book and hit one up. They did have an ad in the book, so they should be good enough, he thought.

The exterminator walked the inside of the trailer. He sprayed corners, under the sink, in the bathrooms, and other dark areas. Greg ran into Billy in his bedroom and made small chit-chat with him before exiting. Erica told Greg before his work not to spray in Billy's room.

Greg made his way outside the trailer, spraying underneath. Erica noticed that he did take a soil sample with him. About twenty minutes later, Greg came back inside.

"Folks," Greg said, "I have to say that your trailer is probably the cleanest one I've ever seen."

Erica was flattered. "Oh, well thank you Greg. I try to keep a good house with my busy schedule."

"Oh, no Mrs. Chandler," Greg replied, "Your house is lovely, but I meant that it is completely roach free."

David and Erica were stunned as they stared at Greg.

"What...did you say?" David asked.

"It's just that I've never been in a trailer so clean where the owners were complaining about roach problems. I never saw one."

"Well that can't be," Erica said. "We see them every day. We step on them at night. We find them in our cereal boxes and on our clean plates. We find them running around on our table, eating holes in our bread. Do you even know what a roach looks like?"

"Mrs. Chandler," Greg said, adjusting his clipboard under his arm, "I've been in this business for fifteen years. I've dealt with the worst of the worst when it comes to roaches. I once walked out of a trailer with about ten roaches clinging to me. So, believe me when I say I know what a roach would look like. Trailer houses are the worst when it comes to collecting roaches and I've seen some horrible ones. Now, I did take a soil sample. We'll examine it in the lab, and I'll call you in a couple of days with the results."

"That's fine," David said, wishing now that he would've done some comparison shopping.

With that, Greg made his departure.

"Can you believe that?" Erica said. "He didn't find any roaches in here?"

Erica walked over to the kitchen and opened the cabinets above the sink. There was no sign of a roach anywhere. "Do you think they all just disappeared?"

"I hope so," David said. "But probably not."

11

The next day, Pam and Richard threw a 4th of July BBQ. David and Erica came over with Billy in tow. Two of Richard's friends, Fred and Janine, made it as well. David and Richard decided to have a 4th of July party every year and that they would take turns. Now that David and Erica had a place of their own, David couldn't wait to have it at his place next year. Surely, he thought, the ghost problem will be a thing of the past by then.

"Glad you could make it bro," Richard said, walking towards the truck, patting David on the back.

"I hope you got that grill fired up," David said, smiling. "Or, do you need my help in getting it started?"

"Very funny," Richard replied. "Can't you smell the wondrous scent of hickory in the air?"

David took a whiff. "Yeah, I'm wondering all right. Smells like burnt hickory to me."

"Boy, you're all fun and jokes today huh?" Richard replied.

"Come on. You can't take a joke? It smells great man."

"Let's go inside and get out of this heat. Besides, I want you to meet some friends of ours."

David and Richard made their way inside. Erica had already gone in with Billy. She took off his brim cap that was keeping the sun out of his face. Pam was sitting in front of the TV as usual when Erica walked in with Billy. Pam lit up when she saw him.

"Come here little Billy!" Pam said, holding out her hands in welcome.

With a big smile on his face, Billy ran into Pam's arms and she hugged him tightly. "I missed you so much."

Erica looked on with concern. She knew the last time Pam had seen him was just yesterday morning, although briefly.

"Erica," Pam said, "this is Janine. She makes the best peanut butter cookies. And this is Fred. He works with Richard."

"Nice to meet both of you," Erica said.

Janine was in the kitchen making her cookies and Fred had just returned from the bathroom when David and Richard burst in the door.

"Fred," Richard said, grabbing his brother from the back of his neck, "this is that bratty brother of mine that I was telling you about."

"Gee thanks Rich," David commented.

"Well," Fred said, "I've heard a lot... about... you. So, you're the one conjuring up spirits."

David looked up surprised, wondering how much Richard had told him.

"I wouldn't call it that Fred," David said softly, trying not to arouse others into the conversation.

Fred placed his hand on David's shoulder as if he was about to offer some friendly advice. "From what I hear, you've got demons living with you." Fred said out loud, followed by a huge grin. "How does your wife like sharing the space?"

Suddenly there was silence as everyone awaited David's response. Pam, worried about Billy's safety, clinched her arms around him more firmly. Erica looked at David, then at Fred who was waiting for an answer.

"They're not living with us," David replied, brushing Fred's arm off his shoulder, "and they're not demons."

"Oh? Then what do you call them?" Fred asked.

"Spirits I suppose," David replied.

Fred looked at Erica, then back at David. "I've dealt with them nasty ones before and let me tell you it isn't pretty. My ex-wife and I lived in a haunted house a few years ago. We heard things we couldn't explain. We saw things that would make anyone go crazy. Objects flying off the shelf; TV turning itself on and off; shadows in the daytime; voices at night speaking in strange tongues. We had this ghost investigator come by and look the place over. And do you know what he said? He told us we had a full-blown poltergeist in that house. Some crazy mess went on in there. We later found out that my ex-wife's uncle lived there years before us and that he died in that house."

Silence filled the room as everyone felt uneasy. Despite the atmosphere, Fred continued. "Her uncle fell down the stairs to his death. I have no doubt that he was haunting the place. My ex-wife didn't agree; of course, she never agreed to anything I had to say. That's one reason why we divorced."

Janine turned her attention back to her cookies in the oven.

Without stopping, Fred kept talking. "She claimed that the ghost produced a strange smell and that her uncle didn't smell like that. He smelled more like Brute Cologne or some crap like that. We didn't agree on anything, you hear me. So, yea, we're talking about demons here. They don't belong in this world."

David jumped in. "Our issue is nothing like what you experienced. We hardly even notice anything going on."

"Demons do different things while they're haunting a place you know," Fred replied. "And what makes matters worse, you summoned them bastards straight to your house using that spirit board."

"I had no idea what that board was capable of," David said, raising his voice. "I didn't do this on purpose. And besides, my knucklehead of a brother was the one who wanted to play the damn thing. I didn't have any intentions of playing it."

"You mean you've never heard of a spirit board and what it can do?" Fred asked.

"No," David replied. "I just thought it was some stupid board game that kids played."

"Right there," Fred replied, his index finger pointed directly at David's face. "It's that kind of stupidity that allows demons to enter this world. If people would get educated on the spirit world and what's out there, then we wouldn't have so many demons walking among us."

"Sure Fred," David said with a smirking grin, "Tomorrow I'll stroll down to the nearest School of Paranormal and get my education in the supernatural."

Richard let out a burst of laughter. "Yeah, you do that bro."

"I think we're making too much out of all this," David said.

"But don't you want these demons out of your house?" Fred asked.

"It's no big deal," David replied. "As I said, we don't experience much of anything in there."

Richard looked at David, knowing he was lying to keep the conversation at bay. Richard thought it would be a good idea to change the subject. He clapped his hands together. "Hey, I think there's a ballgame on. Anyone wanna join?"

Fred turned to Richard. "Count me in!"

And just like that, David was off the hook.

As Fred made his way into the kitchen with Janine, David turned to Richard with a look of anger. "We need to talk later."

Richard nodded, knowing what David meant.

Things calmed down after that with just small chit chat among the group. Janine finished her cookies, and everyone got to try them. As Pam said, they were good. Richard checked in on the grill during the ballgame. When the game reached the 4th inning, the food was ready, and everyone pigged out.

After eating, the ladies pitched in to help clean. Fred took off without bringing up the conversation of ghosts, to David's relief. As David noticed Erica and Pam busy in the kitchen, he walked over to Richard who was sitting on the couch watching the replays.

"Hey, you wanna join me outside?" David asked in a serious tone.

David and Richard walked outside, heading towards the old junk shed where David found the spirit board.

Richard sighed. "I know what this is about. I messed up."

"Damn straight! Why did you tell Fred about our ghosts?" David asked.

"Well," Richard replied, "sometimes we get bored talking about the same thing every day at work. And your situation was the hottest thing on the block."

"Geez Rich," David said, shaking his head. "Please don't mention to anyone else about anything that goes on in our house, especially Fred."

"Ok bro," Richard said. "I didn't think you'd mind."

"Well I do. This is personal. I don't want it getting around town that Erica and I played a spirit board and conjured up demons. I mean, this town isn't that big. It won't take long for word to get around to everyone. And that no-good freelancer will have an article in the Independent in no time. I can just read the headlines now – *"Couple gets answers from the dead using spirit board".* Trust me, that kind of publicity takes years to erase."

"I get it ok," Richard said. "I won't tell another soul about this."

"Good," David replied.

"What did you do with it?"

"With what?" David replied.

"The board."

David looked out into the grassy field. "I threw it outside our house; in the backyard about a week ago."

"Why?"

David turned to Richard, perplexed. "Duh, to get it out of our house. We've got more things going on in that house that I haven't told you about."

"Man, I'm sorry. What happened?"

"I just finished taking a shower and I heard a door slam and then a sound I couldn't make out. I walked the house and then when I returned to the bathroom, the shower had turned itself on. It was scalding water and the room was foggy. It was at that moment I noticed the letters 'out' scrawled on the vanity mirror. I went into our closet and snatched that board, throwing it out the back door."

"Wow!" Richard replied. "That's creepy bro!"

"It just became too much for us. We have a roach infestation, sounds coming from within the house, the sound of a baby crying, and letters spelled out across the mirror. I've had enough."

Richard sat down as to take it all in. "I had no idea all that mess was going on."

David shook his head. "I never thought playing that board would do so much damage."

David sat down next to Richard. "I wish we never touched that thing."

Richard stared at David, a look of sadness. "I agree with you." Richard looked away. "That board has done a number on Pam's thinking."

"Rich, is Pam ok?"

Richard looked down, shaking his head. "No bro, she's not. She's blaming herself for not being able to get pregnant. She believes in that board."

David looked away, thinking. "But it never gave her an exact answer. It just slid off the board."

"Well, to Pam, that was enough."

"I'm sorry Rich. I truly am. Is there anything I can do?"

"I tried getting her to go to the doctor, but she won't, so I didn't know if it was me, or her that was causing a problem with the pregnancy. So, I made an appointment and I had myself checked out."

"What did the doctor say?"

"The doc said that my sperm count was low. Not too low, but under average. He said it was enough of a problem to make conception difficult."

"When was your appointment?"

"Three days ago. I told Pam I was going to work, but I left early to make the appointment. I wanted to be sure it wasn't because of me that we can't get pregnant. As it turns out, it is."

David exhaled. "You haven't told Pam, have you?"

"No."

"Why not?"

"I'm afraid that she'll see me as less of a man. I'm afraid of losing her confidence in me."

"That can't be further from the truth brother. If she loves you, she'll understand. But you have to be honest with her."

"I don't know."

"You have to let her know about this. She's your wife. She deserves to know. You two are in this together. If you go around hiding something this important, it's not going to make the situation any better."

"I know that but telling her may make it worse…for me."

"Let me tell you something." David put his arm around his brother's shoulders. "This feeling that you have about Pam thinking less of you as a man. That's your male ego talking back to you. A lot of guys don't recognize this. You can't listen to it. You don't give your wife enough credit. She agreed to marry you for better or worse. Don't listen to your male ego. She deserves to know."

๛

Pam finished up with the cleaning as Erica was getting Billy ready to go when Pam approached her in the living room.

"So, is it true that your place is haunted?" Pam said, crossing her arms.

Erica finished putting Billy's left shoe on before responding. "David and I sure think so."

"Aren't you worried about Billy's safety?"

Erica rose to meet Pam's eyes. "Well of course I'm worried. Why would you ask that?"

"Well, it seems to me that you would do your best to keep little Billy away from a place that's being haunted by demons."

"Billy is my son. I'll do what I think is right for him. Right now he's not in danger. These spirits or ghosts or demons or whatever you call them have not laid a hand on either one of us, especially Billy. There's no sense in getting all worked up about it."

"If this place was haunted and I had a little boy or girl, I wouldn't dare allow them to stay here until I knew it was safe."

"How do you know what you would or would not do? You don't have a child of your own."

As soon as Erica spoke the words, she remembered the difficulties that Pam was going through. Erica placed her hand over her mouth. "I'm so sorry Pam. I didn't mean to say that. Really."

"It's okay," Pam said, looking down, shaking her head. "You're right. I don't know a damn thing because I've never had a child of my own. You're right."

"It just came out Pam. I truly am sorry about that. I didn't mean any harm. I'm just sick and tired of our ghost problem being the hot topic of conversation all the time."

"Don't worry Erica. I'm fine."

"I think it's time for us to go. We had a wonderful time. I'll drop Billy off tomorrow afternoon."

With a straight face, Pam replied, "That sounds good Erica."

Pam walked back into the kitchen. She watched Erica as she finished putting Billy's right shoe on. Thoughts began to flood Pam's head. She knew that Erica was out of line for what she said. *What does Erica know about keeping a child safe? Not much, supposedly. Why does someone like Erica have the opportunity to raise a child? It's not fair!*

ᶜ

David patted his brother on the back. "So, you gonna tell her about this tonight?"

"Tonight?" Richard asked, shocked. "Why so sudden?"

"Why not?" David replied. "The sooner, the better. Make sure that both of you are alone. Turn the TV off and give her all your attention. Tell her exactly what you told me. Don't sugar coat it. She deserves to know."

"Ok, I'll do it," Richard said. "I knew talking to you about this would help me sort things out."

"I'm glad to be here for you brother. Even though you can be a pain in my backside from time to time."

"Awe," Erica said, walking out on the porch, looking at the brother's bonding. "How sweet."

Richard patted David on the back. "Erica, I have to admit; your husband can be a softy on occasion."

David laughed as he shook his head.

The brothers made their way towards the porch.

"Just some brotherly advice," David said to Erica.

"Well don't let me interrupt you," Erica said.

"Oh, we're done," Richard replied. "That's enough bonding for the day. Are ya'll gone?"

"Yea," Erica said turning to David. "Everything is cleaned up…except for the grill. That's your job Richard."

"Glad to do it," Richard said, looking at the grill with a smile. "First thing in the morning."

As Erica took Billy and put him in the car seat, David and Richard finished up their talk.

"Let me know how things go, ok?" David said.

"I will," Richard said.

"I guess it's back to the ghost house," David said with a sigh.

"Oh, I almost forgot," Richard said. "I was thinking about what you said the other day."

"What's that?" David asked.

"You wondered what dad was so curious about when he took the spirit board. I spoke to dad yesterday about the board."

"What did he say about it?"

Richard shuffled his feet against the ground. "He didn't want to discuss it."

David looked away. "Why not? He didn't say anything?"

"He warned me never to touch it. He made me promise."

David sighed. "Well, it's a little too late for that."

12

1:15 AM

A baby was crying on the other side of the trailer from David and Erica's bedroom. Erica woke up. She could hear the baby crying…almost screaming out in terror. Erica sat in bed, listening to the horrible sounds from the baby boy. It seemed like the cries were getting louder. She almost couldn't stand it any longer. At that moment, she heard a gunshot in the house!

Silence.

The hairs were standing on the back of her neck as she held her ears. She couldn't breathe; she was so frightened by the sound of the gun blast.

Erica jumped out of bed, turning all the lights on in the house as she made her way to Billy's bedroom. When she opened his door, Billy was asleep, as if he didn't hear anything. Erica stood there, watching Billy sleep. For some strange reason, she thought about what it would feel like to shoot and kill a child. *Why was she thinking it?* Tears escaped her eyes as she tried to put the thought out of her head. Erica walked back to her room, shaken up by the sounds she heard. She had had enough. There would be no sleeping tonight.

⁀

"I don't know if we should get more roach spray or not," David said, making out a grocery list the next morning. "It's like the exterminator didn't do anything."

"Well," Erica said, "he also said this was the cleanest trailer he'd ever seen. So how do you kill something that isn't here?"

"But they are here," David said, walking over to the upper cabinets and opening them, releasing dozens of little roaches as if he just cracked open an egg full of them. "This is ridiculous. I'm putting more spray on the list."

"We better get going," Erica said. "We still have to drop Billy off at Pam's. I'm sure everyone in town is at the store by now. It's that time of the day."

"Ready when you are sweetie," David replied.

David noticed Erica staring out the window at the oak tree.

He walked over to her. "Are you ok?"

Erica looked at David, her eyes welling up. "That gunshot last night frightened me. What are we going to do?"

David combed his fingers through her hair and pulled her towards him in a hug. "I don't know sweetie. I'm not sure what to do."

Tears were streaming down Erica's face as she tried to pull herself together.

"Hey," David said, "let me get you some tissue."

David rushed into the bathroom, only to notice there was no toilet tissue. "I think we're out of toilet tissue honey."

Erica wiped her tears from her cheeks. "Check the bedroom closet for some. I knew we were getting low."

As David opened the door, his eyed widened as he stood stone-cold in front of the closet.

Erica noticed David not moving. "Honey, you ok?"

David didn't reply. He was staring at the spirit board; perfectly placed back in their closet in its original box. The smell coming from it was stronger than ever.

"Impossible," David said.

13

An hour had passed since David and Erica left the house for groceries. Arthur Rasberry was busy working in his yard, picking up sticks. He noticed them leave and glanced at the trailer. It had been quiet the past few days and no visitation from David. Arthur knew that once David was ready to talk, he'd be back for answers.

Just minutes later, Arthur watched as an unfamiliar car pulled in the Chandler's driveway. He scurried behind a tree to watch a young girl and guy approach the trailer.

Amanda knocked on the door. "I guess no one is here," Amanda said to her boyfriend Stephen. "And the door is locked so there's no way to get in."

"Allow me," Stephen replied, pulling out a safety pin.

"Those things don't work," Amanda placed her hands on her hips.

"You just never have any faith in me."

Stephen considered himself a magician of sorts. He practiced the art daily. After a few minutes of tinkering, he heard a click. He stood up and turned the knob. The door opened.

"Ladies first," Stephen said, with his chin up.

"Show off."

Stephen stayed in the living room as Amanda walked into her sister's bedroom to retrieve the spirit board. As Amanda made her way back into the living room with the board in her hand, Stephen was stunned by what he saw.

With a look of astonishment, Stephen said, "That's not just some ordinary board. That's a seasoned one."

Amanda placed the board on the table they set up. "It sure has a funky smell too."

"This board is old," Stephen said, looking for a manufacturing date. "1950s. The older the board, the more seasoned it is."

"But why is that?" Amanda asked.

Stephen ran his hand across the top. "This board has been played by many people throughout its existence. It's a tool used to communicate with the spirits who have not yet entered the other side. Countless questions have been asked over this board and the spirits have responded many times. They are familiar with a board like this."

"It probably was bought at a toy store years ago."

Stephen shook his head. "Hardly. If you were to buy a shiny new board right off the shelves, it wouldn't be the same. You may get a response, but not the kind of responses we're about to get from this board."

Not only does Stephen consider himself a novice magician, but he's studying the paranormal during his time at the university. Majoring in demonology, he's learning as much as he can about demons and their origin.

Amanda sat down next to the board. "I can't believe you dragged me into this."

"I couldn't resist after you told me about this board," Stephen replied as he stared down at the board. "I had to see it for myself."

"Who will ask the questions first?" Amanda asked, wanting to get started. "David and Erica may be back soon."

"First things first," Stephen said as he shut off all the lights and pulled the curtains together, blocking off as much light as possible. He wanted to give the room a dark feel.

"Light usually hinders the board's reactions," Stephen said. "That's why it's better to play this puppy at night.

The spirits seem to respond more easily, and their answers are more accurate in the darkness."

Amanda and Stephen sat opposite from each other at the table. With the board unfolded and the planchette in place, the two were ready.

Stephen spoke up. "Ok. We'll take a few moments to clear our minds and get relaxed, so we'll be sensitive to any sensations or vibrations from the board. The spirits feed off this when providing answers. This board is just a medium between us and the spirit world."

"How does this little object move on its own?" Amanda asked.

"The planchette's movement is still unknown. The ideomotor effect says that an individual, who asks the question, makes motions without conscious awareness, drawing on the others who are playing. It's a psychological phenomenon that hasn't been proved yet."

"This board freaks me out," Amanda said.

"The board itself is not dangerous. It's the form of communication that is. Those spirits that are contacted are said to live on the astral plane."

Amanda glanced up at Stephen with a look of crazy in her eyes. "Please repeat."

"These spirits are often confused about who they are and where they should be. They usually have died a violent or sudden death like murder or suicide. It is known that if you ask for proof of their existence, that's when you open a doorway to their world and allow them to come through."

"Come through what?" Amanda asked, looking around.

"That is unknown as well. Some sources say spirits enter and leave a room through mirrors because mirrors are a reflection…a somewhat vortex from the astral plane into the real world…the world in which we live. But that hasn't been proved by natural laws either."

"Why don't we start praying…I mean… playing already," Amanda said, nervously.

Stephen and Amanda took a moment to relax and clear their minds. Then, as Stephen instructed they do, they placed their fingertips on the planchette and moved it around the center of the board in circles, to warm the board up. Then it was time to ask questions.

"Now," Stephen added, "one more thing. If something unusual happens, don't react. Just stay calm and observe what's going on, ok?"

"Well, what if something comes out of this board and grabs you by the throat? You want me to sit here calmly and observe your slow agonizing death?"

Stephen looked at Amanda with a parted smile. "If that happens, you better get me the hell out of here."

Amanda burst out in laughter. "That's what I thought."

"Ok. I'll let you ask the first question."

The two put their fingertips on the planchette and Amanda draws up her first question.

"How many of us are in this room?" Amanda asked.

They waited patiently for the planchette to move. After about a minute, the planchette begins to move and slides on 6.

Amanda looked puzzled. "That can't be right."

Stephen looked up at her. "It's counting the spirits who are already here."

Amanda's eyes widened as she stared at him as if he was joking, but his serious look convinced her otherwise. "What do you mean?"

"You said this board has been played in this house before, right?"

"Yea. So?"

"If something came through, then the spirit board will count them as well."

"Ok, now that freaks me out."

"Ask another question Amanda," Stephen insisted.

"How do you spell my name?" Amanda asked.

The planchette moved over the letters slowly, spelling out Amanda's first and last name correctly."

"Are you moving it?" Amanda asked.

"Of course not," Stephen said in amazement. "Remember our talk on the way here? I swore that I wouldn't move it and I didn't. This board is very seasoned and I'm gonna put it to the test."

"What are you gonna do?" Amanda asked.

"Just put your fingers back on and concentrate. Concentrate hard. Let your mind go at ease and just focus on my question."

Stephen placed his fingers on the planchette as he began to speak slowly to the board. "Listen carefully to the sound of my voice. I know who you are. I know what you are. Tell us your name."

Without hesitation, the planchette slid over to *no*.

"I'm not here to play games," Stephen continued. "You are a spirit living in this house. Tell us your name."

The planchette moved so fast that Amanda and Stephen could barely keep their fingers on it. The planchette moved back to *no*.

"I think you're making it mad," Amanda said.

"Where did you come from? Tell me now," Stephen demanded.

The planchette slid off the board with neither Amanda nor Stephen touching it.

"Holy crap," Amanda said. "I thought that thing only moved if we were touching it."

Stephen hesitated before responding. "That's the general idea. But this is no ordinary board we're dealing with."

Stephen reached down, picked up the planchette and placed it back on the board.

"When the planchette slides off the board like that, it means that a spirit is trying to make its way into the physical world."

Amanda looked confused. "What physical world?"

"Our world…it's trying to get into this house."

"Ok, I'd rather that not happen," Amanda replied. "Let's call it a day, shall we?"

"Hold on. Let me ask one more question."

"Honestly, if you placed that moving device across my gut, it would say we should get the hell out of here before we drag hell into Erica's house."

"Just one more question Amanda. C'mon."

Amanda and Stephen placed their fingertips on the planchette again and Stephen spoke his next question.

"Give me the year, month, and date that I will die," Stephen said.

Amanda was shocked at Stephen's question, but she didn't take her fingers off the planchette. She knew that Stephen would be upset at her if she did. The planchette began to move over letters and numbers and after it was done, the board had predicted when Stephen would die.

"Oh God!" Amanda said, placing her hand over her mouth. "I can't believe you asked that stupid question."

"Wow," Stephen said, "I can't either."

"That was so stupid of you Stephen. Why did you have to ask that question? Now I'm gonna be paranoid about this until then."

"You'll be paranoid? How do you think I feel?"

"Now that you've ruined the rest of the day for us, can we get out of here? Erica and David will be back soon."

"I need to know its name. Put your fingers back on and concentrate."

"Concentrate? How do you expect me to concentrate after that?"

"Just do it! Come on. I'll get its name. Then we can go."

"They have names? Who named them? Their mommy?"

"Knock it off and concentrate Amanda. Please."

Amanda looked at Stephen with concern as she placed her fingers back on the planchette and Stephen asked the question again. "Tell us your name."

The planchette slid to *no*.

"I said tell us your name. If you can predict my death, then I have the right to know who you are. So for the last time damn it, tell us your name."

The planchette made a sudden jerk, then stopped. A gentle breeze blew through the room; enough to cause the curtains to sway back and forth. Chill bumps ran up Amanda's arms as she felt the cold wind against her skin. The planchette made another jerk, then slid upward, then downward. Stephen and Amanda could barely keep their fingers on it. It began spelling a name. Stephen watched as the planchette moved by itself over a series of letters, spelling out the name *Kasdeya*.

Amanda looked on in total confusion. "What does it mean?"

Stephen stared down at the board. "You don't want to know."

"Then humor me, please."

"Kasdeya is from the book of Enoch. It means the 5th Satan."

Just then, the planchette shot off the board, flying across the room and hitting the wall. The mirror behind Amanda cracked down the center and the wind began to pick up.

Stephen and Amanda sat there, looking at each other, frightened.

"Just remain calm and observe," Stephen reminded her.

At that moment, the wind stopped as the front door slammed shut. Stephen and Amanda turned their attention to the hallway as Erica and David walked in with grocery bags in their hands. Erica noticed the spirit board, the cracked mirror, and the planchette sitting on the floor across the room. She remembered Amanda telling her that Stephen was a demonologist. She felt the cold wind cut through her skin like the first touch of a hard winter. The grocery bag left her arms and dropped to the floor.

Erica stared at her sister and calmly asked, "What have you done?"

Amanda stood up. "I'm so sorry Erica."

"How in the hell did you get in?" Erica asked, gritting her teeth.

Stephen stood up. "I'm sorry Mrs. Chandler. It's all my fault. I picked the lock."

David cut in. "You what!?!"

Erica placed her hand across her husband's chest. "Let me handle this David," Erica demanded.

David stepped back, not taking his eyes off Stephen.

"What the hell have you done?" Erica asked.

"We…we were just playing the spirit board," Amanda said, still shaking with her arms folded.

Erica pointed towards the front door. "GET THE HELL OUT OF MY HOUSE NOW!"

Stephen and Amanda headed for the door.

"I'm sorry Erica," Amanda said. "We didn't mean any harm."

Erica grabbed Amanda's arm as she passed by. "What happened here? What did you ask that board?"

Amanda began to cry. "I'm sorry Erica. I'm so sorry."

"Stop saying you're sorry and tell me!" Erica shouted.

Erica could only imagine what went on while she and David were gone. David grabbed the smashed grocery bag and headed into the kitchen, sitting the bags down on the table, smashing a few roaches. Stephen was already outside, waiting for Amanda.

Erica demanded. "What did you ask that board?"

David looked on from the kitchen.

"Stephen wanted to know the spirit's name," Amanda said, looking down at the floor. "That's how your mirror cracked and that triangle thing landed over there. It shot off the board without us touching it."

Erica's eyes widened and David swallowed hard to avoid choking.

"What did the board say?" Erica asked in a low tone of voice.

"Kasdeya," Amanda replied. "That's what the board spelled out."

Erica's eyes widened some more. "What else did you ask the board?"

"Stephen wanted to know when he was gonna die," Amanda said, beginning to cry again.

Erica was curious beyond reason. "Did the board give him an answer?"

Amanda burst out in tears. "Yes."

Erica turned to look at David, who was stunned.

Amanda wiped more tears away. "The board gave an exact date. It said -"

"Go home Amanda," Erica said, letting go of her arm. "I don't care to know."

Amanda and Stephen took off, leaving David and Erica to clean up. Erica picked the planchette off the floor and put it back into the box along with the board. Then she folded up the table, all without saying a word to David.

After putting away the groceries, David finally broke the silence. "I can tell you're thinking about something. What's on your mind?"

Erica didn't say at first. She had a lot of things going through her mind at that point.

David approached Erica. "Talk to me sweetie," he said, looking into her brown eyes.

Erica eyed David. "How did that board get back inside this house after you threw it out?"

David shook his head. "I have no idea."

"Our lives may be in danger now. No telling what came through that board today. We may all be dying here tonight."

David placed his hands around Erica's shoulders. "Don't say that. We'll figure something out."

Erica stood looking at her husband, thinking about the answer to her question. She began to fear the worst.

"You need to get a grip on yourself," David said. "We may need to get some serious help in dealing with these ghosts if it becomes more than we can handle."

"Well, we can just find another place to live."

"We can't sweetie. We just moved here and we don't have enough money to put down on another house. We barely have a savings account right now. We used up most of our money getting here. I hate to say it, but we need to deal with what we got."

"What if I don't want to live in a haunted house?"

"You think I want to? I agree with you that we shouldn't have to put up with all this, but your sister and her demon loving boyfriend didn't help matters today."

"Don't start blaming my sister for this. She didn't know what was going to happen here today. It was Stephen who broke into our house and conjured up no telling what from that damn board."

"I'm just saying…"

"And besides, wasn't it you and Richard who found this board? And wasn't it you who brought it here? We started this mess – not my sister. If matters are worse now, it was because of Stephen."

"That guy has always given me the creeps anyway. Maybe I'll give him the board and let him have a go at it."

"No! You're not giving that board to anyone. My sister lives there too, you know."

David slammed down a loaf of bread on the table. "I was just kidding Erica! I'm pissed off about this. You know me. I'm gonna make comments like that."

Erica took a deep breath. "I'm sorry."

David looked down. "Me too."

Erica folded her arms. "It feels different in here."

"Unsettling? Uninviting?"

Erica nodded her head. "And cold."

David and Erica stared at the spirit board, wondering what their next move should be.

Erica sighed, "I want that board out of our house!"

14

When David had the idea for him and Erica to get a place of their own, he expected to deal with a whole host of problems that came with being a homeowner. He knew the plumbing would give him trouble and perhaps electrical shortages, especially with an older trailer as the one they bought. But never did it cross his mind that he would be dealing with ghosts.

The thought had never occurred to him. It wouldn't occur to anyone who was buying their first home. The excitement he felt of moving in for the first time outweighed all potential issues he'd face regarding a home. But ghosts? That's another problem. But for David, somehow, he felt this coming. It was a feeling he'd felt before moving in. He just couldn't explain it.

⌐

That afternoon, David was outside working on his grass trimmer when he noticed in the corner of his eye, Arthur Rasberry staring at him through the shrubs. David knew that the old man was keeping something from him. He figured right now would be a good time as any to get it all out. Arthur began eyeing the shrubs when he noticed David coming his way.

David said, "Nice day, huh?"

"I suppose," Arthur replied. "We got a little rain coming this evening. Hopefully it'll cool things down."

David looked towards the skies. "Yeah, we sure need some."

Arthur stared at David. "You didn't come here to discuss the weather."

David cleared his throat. "No, I didn't. I came here to finish our last conversation."

"So I figured."

"I'm ready to listen to what you have to say. You told me to come back when I was ready to talk. So, here I am."

Arthur motioned David to step through the shrubs. "Join me over here in the shade."

Arthur made his way underneath a canopy with David behind him. They approached a small outdoor table and chairs. "Take a seat young man. I can tell something is weighing on your mind."

"You might say that," David said, sitting down across from Arthur. "It's been weighing on my mind ever since I set eyes on that trailer."

"Is that right," Arthur replied, pulling up a chair.

David stared at the table and sighed. "Something is troubling me…and my family. We've been dealing with a lot of things lately."

"Things inside that trailer."

David eyed the old man. "Yes. I assume you know what I'm talking about."

"I can tell what's troubling you. Even though I'm unaware of the specifics, I do know for certain that trailer has a curse over it."

David studied the old man. "Our trailer is haunted."

"It took you long enough to admit it. Now we can get somewhere."

David looked away briefly, trying to understand where Arthur was coming from. "It seems to me that you know more about that trailer than I do. How is that?"

Arthur shook his head. "You see Mr. Chandler, I have this unique gift. I could tell that you knew something wasn't right about that trailer the first time we talked. You were going on about how great that trailer was and that your family was loving it. But you were leaving out the part that I already knew. The truth. You wouldn't admit it, so I had nothing else to say to you."

"Why didn't you just come out and tell me?"

"You can't help people who don't want to help themselves Mr. Chandler."

"So, you have a gift."

Arthur nodded. "It's difficult to explain but I have a strong sense of…intuition. It's more powerful than what some people refer to as 'gut feeling'."

"So, you have this ability to tell when something is wrong."

"It's more than that. The feeling I felt when the movers were pulling in with your home was unsettling. The feeling was strong. But, more importantly, I sensed that you felt it as well."

David turned away for a moment. He sighed. "I wasn't completely ok with the trailer when I first looked at it. It seemed that something was…not right about it. I had this negative feeling when I stepped through the front door for the first time. Hell, I still get that feeling now, but it's grown stronger. But, when Erica looked at it, she saw potential. She began telling me how we could paint this and fix that to make it look better. She fell in love with it. Sometimes I think she fell in love with the idea of owning our own place. It was our dream for nearly five years. So, I bought it …for her. To make her happy."

Arthur smiled. "That's understandable. I would've done the same thing. But what you may have done is put your family at risk by buying that trailer."

"Now, let's not jump to conclusions here. You don't know the half of what's going on in that trailer since we bought it. That trailer was perfectly fine until we brought in a spirit board and started playing it."

Arthur leaned back in his chair, taking in a deep breath. "Dear God. That explains a lot."

"Well enlighten me."

"You think playing that spirit board brought those spirits in your home? You couldn't be further from the truth. Those spirits were already inhabiting that trailer. You just provided them with an escape route. You gave them the power to take control of your home."

"I don't understand."

"Those spirits were already there, but they were dormant. They were resting…between this world and the other side. It's like they were trapped between the two planes. Your spirit board allowed them to communicate with you and find their way into this world. Now they're trapped in your home."

"This all sounds like something my brother would come up with."

Arthur stared at David for a moment. "Do you and your wife consider yourselves Christians, Mr. Chandler?"

David was surprised at the question. "Yes, we are. My wife and I are good Christians. What does that have to do with this?"

"Christians don't go around raising the dead. You're doing Satan a favor by bringing those spirits here on Earth."

"That's enough!" David shouted, coming off his chair. "It's not like that at all. Yes, I knew something wasn't right with that trailer before we bought it and it was wrong of us to play that spirit board. We've just got into some trouble and now I don't know if there's a way out of it. But that doesn't give you the right to judge me and my family.

And just to remind you, it is not the duty of Christians to judge; that's the Lord's call to make."

Arthur hesitated before replying. "I'm sorry Mr. Chandler. I owe you an apology. I wish I could help you with your situation, but I can't."

David looked down at the old man. "I didn't expect you to. I thought I could figure this out on my own by talking to you about this. You seemed to know something about that trailer."

"I can tell you this Mr. Chandler. You may have some psychic abilities that you're unaware of. You sensed something wasn't right with that trailer when you first saw it. I would look into that if I was you. As far as your home, I can't advise you with that."

"Other than sensing negativity when I first saw the trailer, why would you think I have those kinds of abilities?"

"Because I'm a bit psychic myself. And psychics can feel each other's energy. You have that same energy as I. It's how I could sense almost exactly what you were feeling towards your home."

"So, now you're telling me that you're a psychic?"

"Not a true psychic. It's something that's always been a part of me."

"How long have you known about this?"

"You mean, what age was I when I discovered this ability? I'd say around thirteen."

David was silent for a moment. "13, huh?"

"You should check into it. It's a nice thing to have, especially when you've worked on it to the point where you can read what other people are thinking. It's an amazing thing. My late wife hated it. On most occasions, I could tell what she was thinking. It made her so mad, bless her heart. But I never used my abilities in a bad way."

"When did she pass away?" David asked.

"Ten years ago," Arthur replied. "She was killed in a car accident. Her and my great-granddaughter Mary."

David returned to his seat, remembering what Richard had told him. "What happened?"

Arthur drew a long breath, looking up into the sky as if gathering his thoughts. "It happened on a dark, rainy night. Elizabeth and Mary were coming back from seeing a play in Natchitoches. Before they reached Jonesboro, they were hit by a drunk driver. They coasted down the hill and into the Dugdemona River. The driver of the 18-wheeler escaped with minor cuts and bruises. But Elizabeth and little Mary were still in the car, with no way to escape. They drowned inside the car before help could arrive." Arthur looked away, hesitating with his words. "The worst day of my life. The memory will stay with me until the Lord calls me home."

David bowed his head. "I'm sorry."

Arthur regained his composure. "That land that you and your family live on was an extension of my land. When it was time for funeral arrangements, I had my land split into two lots. Those dogwood shrubs now grow right down the center. The land that you and your family live on...I sold it to your father. I used the money for the funeral."

David sat in shock. "I didn't know that. Why didn't my dad tell me about this?"

"He and I know each other very well. He's a good man, your father."

"But dad has never mentioned you to me or my brother until...recently."

"I'm sure your father has a lot of friends you don't know about. Your father and I go way back."

David stared at Arthur perplexed, in silence.

"You ok son?" Arthur asked.

David rose from his seat. "I need you to come with me. There's something I want you to see."

In no time, David and Mr. Rasberry were at the trailer. David opened the back door and allowed Arthur to step in.

"Sweetie?" David called out to Erica.

"Coming," Erica replied as she made her way into the living room.

David noticed Arthur acting differently. "Are you ok?"

Arthur shook. "It doesn't feel right inside here Mr. Chandler."

"This won't take long. I promise."

David asked Erica to retrieve the oil painting she finished the other day. When Erica placed the painting in the living room, Mr. Rasberry took one look at it and his mouth nearly dropped to the floor.

"Mr. Rasberry," David said, "my wife painted this picture the other day. This is what she saw looking out the living room window."

Erica stared at Arthur as his eyes welled up with tears. "Is everything ok?" Erica asked.

Arthur stared down at the painting as tears streamed down his face. He slowly kneeled in front of the easel.

Neither Erica nor David knew what to say.

Arthur reached out and touched the painting. He brushed his hand across the woman and child standing next to the oak tree. Then, he spoke in a soft voice. "Mrs. Chandler…my dear…that is my late wife and a great-granddaughter."

15

Arthur sat down on the couch, staring at the painting. "I never thought I'd see them again. They look so beautiful…so peaceful."

Erica was in shock. "So, what happened to them?"

David turned to Erica. "They were killed by a drunk driver."

"O my," Erica replied. "I'm so sorry."

"It's been ten years since I last saw them, but it feels like forever," the old man said, running his hand across the painting. "You have a talent for painting Mrs. Chandler. This picture is most beautiful."

"Thank you," Erica said. "My mom taught me a lot about oil painting."

"She taught you very well," Arthur replied.

He turned to David. "Thank you for sharing this with me. I can't tell you how much this means to me."

David smiled. "I'm glad that we know who they are now."

"They will not harm you or your family," Arthur said. "You shouldn't fear them."

Erica walked toward Arthur. "I've watched them. I could tell that they were very good people."

Arthur smiled. "They truly were." He turned back to the painting. "Well, I best be getting on."

"Arthur," David said, "there's something else I need to show you."

Just as Arthur began walking towards the door, he grabbed his stomach and bent forward.

David grabbed him to keep him from falling. "Arthur?"

Erica cried out. "Oh my God! What's happening?"

The old man dropped to his knees in pain. He tried to speak, but the pain was unbearable.

"Call the hospital!" David shouted to Erica.

"No!" Arthur shouted. He turned to David, pointing to the door. "Just get me out of this house. Now!"

David didn't bother with reason. He quickly picked up the old man and walked out the front door. Erica put down the phone. She looked out the kitchen window at David helped Arthur across the yard.

By the time David had reached the dogwood shrubs, Mr. Rasberry was okay.

"Thank you," Arthur said, breathing heavily. "I feel better now."

"What happened to you back there?" David asked.

"It's that trailer of yours. Every time I get near it, I began to feel this pain inside my stomach. It's like something is trying to get inside of me."

"Wait. You said every time you get near the trailer. How many times have you been over there?"

"This is only the second time. The first time, I thought someone had broken in and I called the police. There's no need to get all upset. We've already agreed that your house is evil."

"Do you think something was trying to hurt you because you're a psychic?"

"I don't think so. I mean, I don't go around practicing the stuff. I have no idea what that was about."

"Neither do I."

Just as Arthur was about to turn and head through the shrubs, he noticed two transparent figures, standing near the trailer. His eyes widened.

"Arthur?" David asked as he turned to look in the direction the old man was looking. He saw nothing.

"I see them," the old man whispered. "They're trying to tell me something."

"What?" David asked, wishing he could see the two figures.

Arthur looked on at his late wife and great-granddaughter, who stood next to each other. His eyes began to water as he focused on Elizabeth, who was trying to communicate with him.

"What are they saying?"

"It's Elizabeth. She's telling me…to stay away…from your house."

"But why?"

Then Arthur looked down, wiping his eyes. "They're gone."

David turned to look back at where the two figures were, then back at Arthur. "Can I do anything for you?"

"No. I need to rest. Just know that your family may be in danger as long as you continue living in that trailer."

Arthur made his way through the shrubs, heading towards his house. David stood there, watching the old man slowly walk to the front door. He didn't know what to think, other than the fact that his family was in danger.

David walked through the front door, heading towards the kitchen. Erica came out of the bedroom. "Are you okay?"

David finished off a full glass of water before responding. "Wow, I was thirsty."

"What happened to Mr. Rasberry?" Erica asked. "Is he okay?"

"Yeah he's fine," David replied, "now that he's away from this place. It seems that someone was trying to keep him away from here. He claims he saw his late wife and great-granddaughter before heading back home."

"Did he see them?"

"So he says. He saw them near the back door. They told him to stay away from this place."

"But why?"

"I don't know anything anymore. All these strange sounds at night and seeing ghosts are about to drive me up the wall."

"Well, we'd better go get Billy from Pam," Erica said, grabbing her purse. "She's had him ever since we left for the store earlier today."

"Yea. Good idea," David replied. "Let me get just one thing."

Erica noticed David walking out of their bedroom with the spirit board in his hand.

"That board has caused us nothing but trouble," Erica said.

"And to think I was about to show this to Arthur," David replied. "He has no idea this is the board he gave to dad years ago."

"It's best he never knows."

"I'm taking this board back where it came from," David said. "Maybe all this crap will stop around here. Let's go."

16

David and Erica arrived at Richard and Pam's.

"I'm sorry it took so long," Erica said, walking in the house.

Pam had the door open and a Sears box fan blowing to circulate cool air in the trailer.

"Nonsense," Pam replied, looking down at Billy. "He's been a sweetheart ever since y'all been gone. Nothing to worry about."

"Thanks," Erica replied. "You've been a really big help today."

"Glad to do it," Pam said.

David joined Richard in the kitchen. David whispered, "Did you talk to Pam about you know what?"

Knowing what David was referring to, Richard shook his head no.

"Why not Rich?"

"I'm sorry bro. I just can't tell her."

"Yes you can. She deserves to know."

"I know that. But it doesn't make it any easier for me."

"Who said it was going to be easy?"

Erica approached them in the kitchen with a big smile on her face. "Why are we talking so quietly over here?"

"Oh nothing," David replied. "Just some brother to brother talk, you know."

Erica gave her husband that 'you're keeping something from me' look.

"Oh, I almost forgot," Richard said to break the silence. "Bro, I need to show you something I found the other day. Walk with me outside to the shed."

"Okay," David replied. "I got something to return anyway."

David looked at Erica as he made his way to the front door. "We'll be outside if you need us sweetie."

"Okay," Erica replied, still wondering what the boys were talking about earlier.

As David and Richard walked outside, Billy ran towards the screen door, watching his dad retrieve the spirit board from the truck. Billy began to cry.

Pam stood up. "Aww, poor Billy. What's the matter?" Pam reached down and lifted him. "You want to go outside with your daddy?"

Billy began pointing towards the junk shed.

Pam turned to Erica. "I think he misses his daddy."

Erica smiled. "I'm sure that's it."

Billy wiggled out of Pam's arms and bolted outside.

"Billy!" Erica called out. "Come back here."

Billy was already off the porch and heading towards the shed.

David turned around with the spirit board in his hand. "Aww, what's the matter little guy?"

Billy reached for the board.

"Whoa Billy," David said, pulling the board from his hands. "This isn't a toy." David looked up at Erica as she arrived and scooped Billy up.

David stared at Erica. "What's gotten into Billy?"

Erica didn't reply, only shaking her head.

Richard chimed in. "It looks like little Billy wants to play the board game."

David looked over at Richard, a look of shock on his face. "This isn't a game, Rich. And it's going back where I found it."

"I know bro," Richard replied. "But Billy doesn't"

"Billy has never seen this board before. What's gotten into him?"

Erica began walking back to the porch with Billy in her arms. Billy was looking back at David and the board, still sobbing.

Erica sat Billy down in one of the porch rockers. Pam stood in the doorway, concerned.

"Billy," Erica said, "what's the matter?"

Billy rubbed his eyes as he was calming down. "Wee jee."

Erica stared silently at Billy. She turned to Pam, who had a surprising look on her face. Erica replied, "Billy, what do you know about Ouija?"

Billy locked eyes with his mom. "They...want... it back."

Shocked by his response, Erica was speechless.

Pam stared at Erica, a convicting look in her eyes.

e

David opened the door to the junk shed, breathing in the smell of antiques and years of settled dust. "Come on now," David said. "You've got to tell Pam what's going on here. You can't keep this a secret forever."

"I'd feel better that way," Richard replied.

David walked to the back of the shed and placed the spirit board on the top shelf. "You're something else, you know that. I would never keep a secret like this from Erica."

Richard watched as David gave the board a shove to the back of the shelf. "You're done with the board, huh?"

David scoffed. "I should've never touched it in the first place. There's no telling what damage we've done by playing with it."

David waited for a response. "Do you want it Rich? Do you wanna take this board and shove it in your closet and sit back while your house gets taken over by spirits?"

"No of course not," Richard replied quickly. "Leave it there. Maybe it'll drive the rats away now that you've woke it up."

"Very funny," David replied as he sighed in relief of walking away from it. "There's things I haven't told you yet; the trouble that board has caused."

"What's been going on, bro?"

"I talked to Arthur Rasberry today. He told me the story of how his wife and great-granddaughter died. Well, the other day, Erica showed me a painting she did; it was a silhouette of an older woman and child standing near our oak tree in the back yard."

"Oh, that's crazy," Richard replied.

"Well, on a hunch, I invited Mr. Rasberry over to the house and Erica showed him the painting."

"And?"

"Brother, I'm telling you that old man dropped to his knees after seeing that painting. He told us that was his late wife and great-granddaughter, Mary."

Richard looked away in astonishment. "I can't believe it."

"Just minutes after talking about the painting, Mr. Rasberry fell ill inside our house. He told me to get him out. He couldn't take any longer."

"Did something have a hold on him?"

"I'm not sure, but he said our house gives him that sick feeling inside. I'm telling you, that board is dangerous."

"Well, I certainly don't want that board after what I heard from daddy yesterday."

David shut the door to the junk shed. "You talked to Dad about the spirit board again?"

"Yeah, and I told him I lied and that we been playing with it and that you had it at your house."

"Oh boy. What did he say about it?"

"A lot bro. A lot."

⸎

Billy had calmed down as Erica was trying to get him ready to go, but he wanted to keep playing with his army toys.

"He can be stubborn sometimes," Erica said.

"Awe," Pam replied, "he's just a kid. Let him play for a few more minutes. It'll give us some time to talk."

Erica stared at Pam before replying. "Did you want to talk some more about you and Richard?"

"No," Pam shot back quickly. "I'm tired of talking about my inability to get pregnant. And I'm not up for hearing any of your faith-based positivity."

Erica considered it a slap in the face when Pam spoke those words.

"Pam, I said that I was sorry about that," Erica said.

"Sorry about what?" Pam asked.

"Don't worry about it," Erica replied. "I thought you said you wanted to talk."

Pam looked at Erica. "How's everything going at your haunted house?"

Erica wasn't in the mood to talk about the hauntings inside her and David's home, especially after what just happened earlier with Mr. Rasberry. "Oh, we're still hearing sounds at night. Sometimes we can hear a baby crying, but it's not Billy. The crying stops when we get to Billy's room."

"That's strange," Pam said. "What are you going to do about all that?"

"I don't know. David and I don't talk about it that much."

"You mean all those sounds you're hearing at night don't bother you?"

"Not really. They're just sounds. What harm can they do?"

"I would be scared out of my wits. I would have a priest over there exorcising that home up and down to get rid of those ghosts. Aren't you worried about Billy's safety?"

"You've asked me that before. I told you that Billy is in no danger. No one is. They're just sounds."

"What if it becomes more? What if it starts threatening?"

Erica knew that the threats were already present. But she didn't want Pam to know about them. For one thing, it's not her business to know. She would also make a big deal about Billy's safety – more than a big deal than what she's making already. Erica figured the less she tells Pam, the better.

Erica picked up Billy to leave abruptly. "Look, Pam. I don't want to talk about this subject. Can we please just drop it?"

"You want to forget about it like it's not even there?" Pam asked, walking with Erica towards the front door. Her eyes on Billy the whole time.

"I'm not in denial about it if that's what you're wondering," Erica said. "I just don't want to discuss it right now."

~

Richard took a seat outside the junk shed. "I wanted to know if dad had asked the board some questions years ago when he first got it and he told me he did. I asked him about the questions, and he hesitated like he didn't want to tell me."

"Why would he hesitate?" David asked.

"He said that the answers may not be true and that no one should know too much about their destiny. He was freaking me out because I've never heard him talk like that before."

"Did he ever tell you what those questions were?"

"Yeah he did, but I want you to agree with me that that board is not always right."

David thought for a second. "Yes…I agree with you."

Richard hesitated.

"So, are you going to tell me or not?"

"Ok. When daddy played the board, he was about our age. He and mom were living here, and she was pregnant with you. At the time, they didn't know the sex of their baby. Mom was only about two months pregnant. Well, when daddy got the board from Mr. Rasberry, the big question on his mind was what kind of child they would have."

"Now why would he want to know the sex of the baby?" David asked. "Erica wanted to know the same thing, but I stopped her from asking."

"O my God!" Richard shouted. "Erica is pregnant?"

"No silly. She asked the board if we were gonna have another child and the board said yes. Then, she started to ask the board what the sex of the baby would be and I stopped her. I didn't want to know what we were having before it was even conceived. That's just weird."

"Well, daddy didn't think so. He asked the board and it said that mom would have two sons from separate births."

David was stunned. "Wow. Really?"

"Yes. Daddy was also curious about grandkids. He asked the board and it said that one of his sons and his future wife would bear a son and the other would bear a daughter."

"Unbelievable."

Richard was smiling. "Seriously. That's why I haven't told Pam about me. We're gonna have a baby girl!"

David didn't know whether to be happy for his brother or be scared out of his mind at the board's predictions.

"Listen to yourself," David said. "You're saying that you believe that board. You just told me to agree with you that the board is not always right. You're contradicting yourself."

"No, I'm not!" Richard shouted.

"C'mon. You're hiding behind that board so you won't have to tell Pam the truth about your inability to father a child."

Richard, furious at David, shoved him out of his chair. David fell back on the concrete. He looked up at Richard, who had an angry look upon his face; a look David hadn't seen in years.

"I didn't think you had it in ya," David said. "I must have hit a nerve."

"I'm sorry about that," Richard said, reaching down to help his brother up. "I was out of line there."

"I'm sorry too," David replied. "I wasn't thinking."

"It's just that...I've never had to deal with something like this and I suck at it. And once I found out what that board said many years ago, I had this relief come over me."

"But you can't believe it's true. You can't go by what some board game said years ago. Yes, some things did come true. But it's just mere coincidence. That's all."

Richard sat back down in the chair. "I know I have to tell Pam the truth."

"Was that all the questions dad asked the board?"

Richard looked up at David for a few seconds. "No. There was another question that daddy promised me not to tell you."

David was stunned as he sat in the chair next to Richard. "What? He doesn't want me to know. Why?"

Just then, Erica calls out from the front porch. "David!"

David rises from his chair. He could see Erica standing on the top step of the porch holding Billy's hand. "Erica, everything ok?"

"We need to go," Erica replied. "We need to get Billy home."

David nodded and looked back at Richard. "What was the question?"

Richard came closer. "Bro, the board predicted something about you and Erica."

"Tell me."

Richard took a deep breath. "Daddy told me that he asked a lot of questions about you and me. He said he was hooked."

"I don't doubt it."

"He told me that through a series of questions regarding you, the board predicted that you and your family would be plagued by ghosts."

David looked towards the sky. "Christ Sakes."

Richard replied, "He and mom played that board game a lot. Mom was just as hooked on it as he was."

David lowered his head.

"I'm sorry bro," Richard said. "Remember, you agreed with me about the board not always being right."

"I know," David said, lifting his head. "But look at what the board has been right about so far. The death of Mr. Rasberry's wife, our parents having two sons, and the questions we asked the board that evening. The board was right about everything. I mean, it's hard not to think otherwise."

"Maybe I shouldn't have told you."

"Did dad say if it was a happy ending by any chance?"

Richard couldn't help but grin. "He and mom thought it was just for fun bro. They didn't question it further."

David shook his head. "Wonderful."

17

David and Erica sat outside on their deck that still smelled of fresh stain. David turned to Erica, "Rich mentioned that we should talk to the previous owners of the house."

Staring across the sky, Erica turned her attention to David. "Why?"

"To get answers, or at least to find out who or what is haunting our house."

"And you're considering this?"

David shrugged his shoulders. "It couldn't hurt."

"I don't know," Erica turned away. "We could come across as two nut jobs. What if they have no idea what we're talking about?"

"I think it's worth a shot," David replied, taking a sip of tea. "Tomorrow is Saturday. We could have Pam watch Billy for us."

Erica looked down. "About that."

David waited for more.

Erica looked at David. "I think we should consider that idea of finding a new babysitter."

"What happened?"

"While you and Richard were in the junk shed, Pam voiced her concern about Billy's safety again. She's also concerned that we're not taking the issue of living with ghosts seriously."

"Well, that's understandable. I mean, she does have a close relationship with Billy."

"That's what concerns me, her close relationship. I'm worried that it will conflict with the fact that she can't have children. She's made her feelings well known to me."

David sighed. "It's not Pam who can't conceive."

Erica stared at David for a moment.

"Richard promised me not to tell anyone. Hopefully, he's told Pam by now."

"Told her what?"

"He went to see a doctor about it. His doctor confirmed it he has a low sperm count and that it makes conception difficult."

"Oh no," Erica replied. "I hate that."

"The thing is, he's too bull-headed to tell her the truth. He also believes that the board is right about him and Pam bearing a daughter in the future."

Erica looked away for a moment. "I don't recall that being one of the questions we all asked that night."

"You're right," David replied. "My parents played that board years ago and it said Richard and his future wife would bear a daughter."

"Oh geez." Erica rubbed her forehead in frustration. "So, he's holding out on her in hopes that the board is right?"

"I'm afraid so."

"Oh no. He's got to tell her because until he does, Pam will always fear for Billy's life and I'm afraid to leave him with her."

"I hardly believe that Pam would hurt Billy."

"I know. I agree. I just have this feeling in me that disagrees."

"You think that Pam could harm Billy in some way?"

"I'm not sure. Perhaps she couldn't hurt him, but...I don't know. I just have this bad feeling. It's the way she expresses her concern for Billy and the ignorance of our living situation; not to mention the fact that she doesn't have a child of her own."

"I sure hope Rich tells her soon."

"Look, I'm all for tracking down the original owners, but what about Billy?"

David stared out into the trees for a moment. "I honestly believe that Pam would be okay with watching Billy for just a few hours."

Erica stared at David. "I hope you're right."

"Me too." David looked out into the yard. "It still bugs me to this day."

"What's that," Erica replied.

"I threw that board out in the yard last week. And somehow, it ends up back in our closet."

Erica looked away.

"It bothers me for some reason."

"There's something else you should know."

David turned back to Erica. "What is it?"

Erica sighed deeply. "When we were at Pam and Richard's when Billy was having his tantrum, he said something to me that threw me off."

"Billy was reaching for the board," David said. "It's like he wanted it. I remember that. What did he say?"

Erica stared at David. "He said Ouija."

David's eyes widened. He didn't reply.

"I asked Billy what he knew about Ouija. He just said, 'they want it back.'"

David continued his blank stare at Erica. "They."

Erica looked away. "What if Billy had something to do with that board coming back inside?"

"I'm afraid to know."

꙳

4:12 AM

David woke up, hearing a baby crying out in terror. He shook Erica.

"Wake up sweetie," David whispered. "You hear that?"

Erica woke, hearing the baby boy crying. "Yeah I've heard this before."

"I'm gonna get up and walk into the living room."

"No!" Erica said, grabbing onto David's arm. "Just lie here for a moment. I want you to hear this."

"What about Billy?"

"Just a second."

David eased back into the bed, listening to the baby cry out. The baby was crying so loud it was becoming hoarse. David and Erica could hardly stand it. Then, there was a gunshot. David nearly jumped straight up. Everything went silent.

David turned to Erica. "My God! That shot was in the house!"

"I know," Erica replied. "It's as if someone shot that baby boy. I cringe every time I think about it."

David's heart was beating rapidly as he got up with Erica to check on Billy, who had slept through the whole event.

David pulled Billy's door closed. "How could Billy sleep through that?"

Erica shook her head in silence.

David had chill bumps on his arms and legs. They listened closely, trying to hear anything else. There was only silence. They made their way back to bed, only they didn't sleep much afterward. They looked forward to in the morning when they speak to the previous owners and hopefully get answers. They had no idea what awaited them.

18

As David and Erica traveled down highway 167 heading west out of town, they pondered on what questions to ask the previous owners. The idea of starting the conversation off with their experiences of seeing ghosts and hearing things at night didn't seem like a good one. David and Erica talked about how to approach them. They knew the previous owners would already be curious as to why they're visiting in the first place.

As they turned off the highway and onto the familiar dirt road, David remembered how he felt when he saw the trailer for the first time. His anticipation and excitement of owning his first home had consumed him. But now, as they traveled down this same dirt road, David began wondering if they made a mistake of buying the trailer. He certainly felt it; believing if the house wasn't haunted in the first place, then the spirit board wouldn't have anything to conjure up.

David and Erica pulled into the driveway and parked behind the minivan sitting in the yard. They got out of the truck, noticing a brand new doublewide mobile home sitting where the trailer once was.

"So," David said, "this is what they traded up to."

"It's beautiful," Erica replied.

Erica noticed acres of cleared land behind the new trailer. There was a tin barn out to the right of the house with an old Ford tractor parked beside it. The ground was soggy; much like the dirt road due to last night's rain. David and Erica walked up on the front porch and a man opened the door before they could get to it.

"Can I help you folks?" The man asked.

"My name is David Chandler and this is my wife Erica. We bought the trailer you and your wife once lived in."

"Oh, yes," the man said. "Now I remember. Come in, want you?"

"Thank you," Erica replied. She noticed that the trailer still had that new home smell to it. "This is beautiful."

"I'll tell Annie you said so," the man said. "All the decorating credit goes to her. Sit down, please. Can I get you anything to drink?"

"Nothing for me," David replied. "Erica?"

"I'm good. Thanks."

David had filled Erica in on what he knew about the Radcliff's on their way there. Chip and Annie Radcliff moved to Jonesboro in the summer of 1965. Chip started an agriculture business raising chickens. Annie had a sewing business in the trailer, making quilts, much like David and Richard's mom. Over the years, Chip's agriculture business began slowing down, due to other chicken farms popping up around the area. In 1982, an oil company came through with an offer for the Radcliff's to sell fifty acres of their land for oil exploration. Chip and Annie decided to sell and later sold the trailer to the Chandler's at an affordable price.

"So, what brings you here today?" Chip asked, taking a sip of his drink.

David glanced at Erica, then back at Chip. "What can you tell us about your experiences living in that trailer you sold us," David asked.

"Well," Chip said, thinking about it for a moment. "What exactly do you want to know about?

"Well," David replied, turning to Erica. "Anything you could tell us."

Chip partly smiled. "Our personal life, social upbringing, or life as a chicken grower?"

David wasn't sure how to ask the question. He turned and looked at Erica again for help. She lightly shrugged her shoulders.

David turned back to Chip, ready to give it to him straight. "Did you or your wife ever experience something unusual in that trailer?"

Chip stared at David for a second. "Unusual…in what way?"

"I don't know," David replied. "Just anything that seemed unusual."

Chip had a confused look on his face. David could tell at that point that if Chip and Annie experienced something in that trailer, he would know exactly what he meant. David wasn't getting any vibe from Chip holding out on anything.

"Let me see if I'm on the same page here," Chip said, leaning up from his chair. "Because I think you want to tell me something, but you're not sure how to say it. Is that right?"

"Yes sir," David said.

"Ok," Chip replied. "The answer is no. My wife and I didn't experience anything unusual while we were living in that trailer."

David looked at Erica. He could tell she was not satisfied with Chip's answer. At that moment, Erica spoke up.

"We think our trailer is haunted."

Chip's eyes widened. "Haunted?"

"We don't think," Erica said, looking at David, "we know."

Chip let the information sink in for a bit before responding. "Are you sure?"

"Yes," David said, "we're sure. We've heard too many things that we can't explain. We've both experienced writing on mirrors, asking us to leave the house. We've seen shadows and figures in the corner of our eyes; our rocking chair moving with no one in it. There are too many things going on in that trailer for us not to believe that it's haunted."

Erica chimed in. "We came here today hoping that you had experienced something in that trailer; something that you would like to share with us."

Chip settled back into his chair. "I wish I had something to share with you folks. But I don't. Annie and I lived in that trailer for eight years and we didn't hear a peep. We didn't see anything that couldn't be explained. I don't know what to tell you about your situation. Personally, I've never experienced anything ghost-related in my life. I don't know…maybe the ghosts are scared of me." Chip erupted with a burst of laughter.

David and Erica just smiled. They didn't find his humor very funny at that moment.

Chip cleared his throat, returning with a serious stare. "And I can speak for Annie in saying that she's never seen or heard anything while living in that trailer either. I don't know what to say other than that."

David and Erica were disappointed. They came to get answers and ended up with nothing.

"Well," David said, "thanks for your time anyway. We should be going." David and Erica rose from their seats.

"Not a problem," Chip replied, walking them to the front door. "I'm sorry you drove all the way here for nothing. I wish I could give you something to go on, but…"

Annie entered the room. "Our guests are already leaving?"

Chip turned around. "Yes, dear. They had some questions about the trailer we sold them."

"Oh?"

Chip turned to David and Erica. "This is my wife, Annie."

David nodded as Erica smiled. "It's nice to meet you," Erica said. "Your home is lovely."

"Thank you," Annie. "Me and Chip do our best. I hate that y'all have to rush off."

Chip replied, "I couldn't help them. They were hoping that you and I had experienced anything unusual about the place while living there."

Annie thought for a moment. "Well, no we certainly didn't."

Chip returned to David and Erica. "I'm sorry it was a dead-end for you."

"Wait!" Annie replied. "Chip, dear, you've got that lady's contact number still, don't you? Perhaps she could help them."

Chip thought for a moment. "Yes, I believe I do." He turned back to David. "Wait just a moment. I may be able to help you after all."

"Yes," David replied, "thank you." David turned to Erica who both seemed to have hope.

Chip walked into the kitchen and began shuffling through a drawer. David and Erica looked at each other, hoping that Chip had remembered something. Just then, Chip returned with a piece of paper.

"Take this," Chip said, giving the paper to David.

David took the paper from his hand.

"This is the lady my wife and I bought the trailer from in 1978," Chip said. "Her name is Rebecca Morris. She lived with the original owners. That's her address. She lives here in Jonesboro. Talk to her about it because I tell you, she sold it to us dirt cheap. A fairly new trailer...dirt cheap. She was desperate to get rid of it."

David looked at Chip. "Did you ask her why she was so desperate to sell?"

"Of course not," Chip replied. "For we were desperate to buy. We needed a roof over our heads after the tornado nearly tore our old home apart."

"This will help us," Erica replied. "Thank you so much for this."

"Yes, thank you," David said. "This may be what we're looking for."

"I hope you find answers," Chip replied, as he said goodbye to the Chandler's.

David and Erica couldn't get across town fast enough. They both had a strong feeling that Rebecca Morris held the key to the answers they were seeking. It only took them fifteen minutes to get to the address they were given.

"What are we gonna say?" Erica asked. "She doesn't even know us."

"We'll just come out and ask her about the trailer," David replied. "No more of this beating around the bush routine. I'm determined to get answers. That trailer had to be haunted before we moved in. I had this feeling inside me when I first looked at it."

"A feeling?" Erica asked. "You never told me about this feeling."

"I didn't think there was anything to it. I just had a suspicious feeling that something wasn't right about the trailer. That's all."

"Why didn't you tell me about this?"

"Because you fell in love with the trailer, sweetie. I wasn't going to ruin it just because I felt something unusual. Who am I to take away your happiness over something I thought was so small?"

"You could've at least told me about it."

"Would it have made a difference? Would you have liked the trailer a little less if I did?"

Erica shrugged her shoulders. "Probably not."

"That's why I didn't say anything. Who knew it would turn out to be haunted?"

As they pulled into the driveway, they noticed the small cottage home and the two-door sedan sitting off to the side. Best guess...she lives alone. Off to the right of the house, was a little shop that looked like a hair salon.

"I bet she's a hairdresser," David said, pulling up behind her car.

"I wonder what her rates are," Erica asked.

"You can ask her about them after we get our answers," David replied.

They walked up to the door and knocked. No one responded. David scanned the yard and the surrounding area. A crow flew over the land, squawking. "It's quiet around here."

"She's not home?" Erica asked, standing behind David.

David knocked again. Still, no answer. "I don't believe this," David said.

Just then, a slender woman stepped out from behind the house. "Can I help you?" the woman asked. She wore a long blue skirt and a cream-colored blouse. She had on a pair of garden gloves that she was removing.

"Are you Rebecca Morris?" David asked.

"That's me," Rebecca replied.

"We were wondering if we could have a few minutes of your time," David asked.

Rebecca eyed the two for a second. "Are you selling salvation or something? What's this all about?"

"No," Erica said. "We're not salesmen. We just want to talk to you for a few minutes, if that's ok."

"Who are you?" Rebecca asked, still standing next to the corner of her house.

"My name is Erica Chandler and this is my husband David. We live here in Jonesboro. We just want to talk with you about something if you can spare a few minutes. I promise this won't take long."

"Ok," Rebecca said, approaching them, still eyeing them suspiciously. "Come inside. We'll talk there."

The three of them walked inside. The living area was nice and cozy. Erica noticed several bookshelves packed with books. She seen an encyclopedia set in the corner behind her rocking chair.

"Do you collect books?" Erica asked.

Rebecca snapped a glance at Erica. "I love to read. It's my favorite pastime…next to my hair salon."

"Oh," Erica said, "we were wondering if you cut hair."

"Yes," Rebecca replied. "For over ten years now."

"Your place is nice," David said.

"It's just the way I like it," Rebecca said, sternly. "Plain, simple and cozy." Rebecca wiped her hands down with a towel. "And quiet." She sat down in her rocking chair.

Feeling a little uneasy, David and Erica sat on the couch across the room. "Look," Rebecca added, "I enjoy chit chat just as much as the next gal, but today is the first day I've felt like getting out in the garden and I wanted to plant some tulips around the house and do some other yard work as well. So, if we could speed this up, I would appreciate it."

"I'm sorry if we disturbed you, Ms. Morris," David said.

"It's quite alright," Rebecca said, "I don't' mean any disrespect, but I would like to keep this short."

David remembered that earlier he told Erica that he wasn't gonna beat around the bush. He was going for the kill to get the answers he needed. David quickly gathered his thoughts.

"Erica and I purchased a trailer you once lived in. We bought it from Chip and Annie Radcliff. I'm sure you know which trailer I'm talking about."

The look on Rebecca's face changed from tranquil to a darken overcast of dread at the thought of the trailer she once lived in. She replied in a somber voice, "Yes, I remember that trailer."

Rebecca didn't say anything else. Her train of thought drifted off as if her memory was feeding her a horrible nightmare she once lived through. David and Erica waited for Rebecca to respond, but she never did.

David cleared his throat, wondering if he should speak. "Can you tell us how it was like living in that trailer?"

Rebecca shot a deep stare through David that made the hairs on his arms curl up. "Why did you come to me today wanting to know about something that happened years ago?"

Erica cut in. "We live in that trailer now. Did something happen in that trailer while you were living there?"

"That's none of your damn business!" Rebecca shouted, standing up from her chair. "Now get the hell out of my house! How dare you come to me and dig up these horrible memories for me to dwell on."

David stood up. "Because we're dealing with them ourselves. They're our problem and we just want answers. Now, I'm sorry if this is painful for you, but we're desperate here. And I feel my family is in danger and we can't afford to just move again."

Rebecca sat down. "You have no idea how painful this was to me," she replied. "If you knew what I went through, then you would leave it alone."

"But we can't," David said. "We need to know what we're dealing with in that house."

Rebecca looked at David confused. "What in the hell are you talking about? What I experienced, happened nearly ten years ago."

Erica stood up. "The trailer is haunted."

Rebecca froze, eyes widened. "Haunted?"

"Yes," David replied. "You're practically admitting that you went through the same thing as my family."

Rebecca was shocked from hearing what the Chandler's were saying. She leaned back in her chair, staring into the dark corner of the room. "Sit down," Rebecca said. "I never experienced a haunting in that trailer."

David and Erica turned to each other. David looked back at Rebecca. "But you mentioned horrible memories. What are you talking about?"

Rebecca sat quietly for a moment, allowing her memory to come back to her. It didn't take long for the horrible memories to resurface. She dreaded the fact that she would have to retell this terrifying event, but she knew it was necessary. She wanted to help David and Erica. She wanted them to know what they were facing.

"I was living with my sister Angela," Rebecca began. "We were living together in a two-bedroom apartment uptown. My sister was married to Abbot Brown, who was active in the Vietnam War since 1965. When Abbot returned in the summer of '73, he and Angela bought a new trailer house, a 1973 single wide Fleetwood…the trailer you live in now."

David felt a sudden chill run down the back of his neck at the thought of the trailer.

"Angela and Abbot were high school sweethearts," Rebecca said. "Their relationship was solid. It was a good one. When Abbot was drafted into the war, he was scared, but he also wanted his future children to grow up knowing he was a hero. That was his big thing when he left for the war. My sister talked about all these plans after he returns; a big family; a big house; that bass boat that Abbot always wanted. They had so many plans. But that's not how it ended up."

David and Erica looked at each other, frightened.

"Angela wanted me to move in with them until I could afford a place of my own, so I accepted her offer. I mean, I didn't have much of a choice."

Rebecca paused for a moment, running her fingers through her hair as David and Erica hung on to every word she was saying. Rebecca turned to her left, towards a bookshelf.

"Angela and I noticed that Abbot wasn't the same upon his return. We first noticed that he was very distant. He would sit by himself for a couple of hours in silence. We just thought that he was trying to readjust to everyday life."

Rebecca turned toward David and Erica. "But later, he started having these awful nightmares where he would wake up screaming in the middle of the night. He would take cover under the bed sometimes as if he was hiding from someone. He told us that he dreamed of walking through the jungles with his platoon. Then suddenly, bombs began dropping and they were running for their lives. He told us about one of his good friends who was killed during a surprise attack, an explosion. He said that he found his friend in bits and pieces, scattered across the jungle. He would go into details, gory descriptions of his battles.

David noticed Erica becoming unsettling; her hands cupped over her mouth.

"Later, Abbot started having terrible headaches all the time. He became more depressed and he just didn't have any ambition for anything in his life. But worst of all, he took up drinking to numb the pain and erase the nightmares. And not just beer. I'm talking about hard liquor. He became dependent on it. He was drunk every weekend it seemed. Angela and Abbot would argue over his excessive drinking and those arguments would usually end where Angela would get pushed down or slapped in the face. Abbot became abusive towards her. He even threatened me at times. Then one day, Angela announced that she was pregnant. When Abbot found out, he was excited, and we started seeing a change in his everyday behavior. He didn't drink as much either. He talked about being a hero in the eyes of his child. Abbot and Angela began discussing those dreams they once talked about."

Rebecca went silent for a moment. David and Erica glanced at each other as Rebecca seemed far away.

"But then, he started telling us war stories again; yet, he seemed less scatterbrained as he spoke. He told us many times about his experiences and living conditions during combat. He talked about their trek through the jungles and the biting insects and torrential rainfalls day and night. He would be soaking wet for days before drying out. The heat and humidity were a problem. The gun fires and bomb blasts that woke him up in the middle of the night led to sleep deprivation. Even though Abbot was home, and the war was over, his mind was still deep in those jungles, still fighting…waiting for the next bomb to drop. Angela finally convinced him to see a counselor. After a couple of visits, the counselor said he was suffering from Chronic Post-Traumatic Stress Disorder…a mental disease. Years of exposure to jungle warfare had led to his mental breakdown. Then, Abbot began skipping his meetings with the counselor after she advised him to see a psychotherapist. He refused medical help. He turned back to alcohol very heavily and that just made matters worse."

David and Erica were speechless as Rebecca continued. Rebecca became quiet, her thoughts on that horrible night she lived through. She wiped the tears from her eyes and continued. "It was horrible living in that place, watching my sister get abused by him. I could never begin to imagine what Abbot went through during the seven years he was in combat, but he didn't want to help himself, not even for his family. After their baby boy Casey was born, my sister and I didn't notice a change in him. He had got to the point where he couldn't change. The nightmares, the distance he placed from his family and the drinking. It continued."

David felt the urge to stop Rebecca from telling any more of the story, but he was desperate for answers, but he hesitated as Rebecca continued.

"Then one evening, I left the house to hang out with some old friends. I just wanted a break from all the craziness around the house. As I was leaving, Abbot was in the corner of the room, sitting in his rocking chair. He was silent as if he was the only person in the house. I didn't even say bye to him. I ended up staying past one that morning. I decided to drive home instead of crashing at my friend's place. When I got home, I unlocked the door and walked into the living room. I turned on the lights… and I saw Abbot's body lying face down on the floor, a hole through his head. A double-barreled shotgun laid next to him. I was too much in shock to scream. All the blood plastered on the furniture and the walls, Abbot's dead body. I could barely stand up. I made my way into my sister's bedroom and found her in bed. She had been shot in the head. I dropped to my knees at the sight of my sister. Quickly my thoughts went to little Casey. I rushed into his bedroom; he, too, had been shot in the head."

Tears streamed down Erica's face. David placed his arm around her.

"I tell you…there was nothing left of his face. You couldn't even tell who he was. His baby crib was covered in crimson red. His lifeless body just laid there in the small crib…"

Rebecca placed her hands over her face. "I'm sorry. The memories…it's horrible to think about."

David looked over at Erica; tears streaming down her face. David reached over and wiped them away.

Rebecca looked up at David and Erica. "The police said that Abbot's prints were on the gun. No one else had touched it. My sister and little nephew were killed by that creep and then he committed suicide. I'll never forget that night."

Erica took in deep breaths and regained composure. "I'm so sorry for what you went through."

"Me too," David said, in a soft voice. "I can't imagine going through something like that." His thoughts were on the sounds they heard last night; the baby crying, the gunshot.

"But you do understand why I couldn't live there?" Rebecca replied. "Why I sold the place so cheap? I didn't want to see that trailer ever again."

David and Erica both nodded in agreement.

Erica replied, "You don't have to tell us anymore."

Rebecca wiped her nose. "There's not much more to tell. If that trailer is haunted, I can assure you it is the ghost of Abbot Brown."

David and Erica looked at each other.

"I hope I've helped you today," Rebecca said.

David turned to her. "More than you know." He reached over and held onto Erica's hand.

உ

David sat in the security booth that night at work; looking out the small window towards the road as the cars drove by; a cup of coffee in front of him and a car magazine opened halfway. His thoughts about the conversation he and Erica had with Rebecca replayed in his mind; he thought about it hard. He was scared for his family.

The sun was beginning to rise. Just then, the dayshift guard stormed in, bringing David back to reality.

"Man," his co-worker spoke up, "you got something riding heavy on your mind."

Without any hesitation, David replied, "Do you believe in ghosts?"

The guard stopped in his tracks. "Do I believe in ghosts? I certainly do. Why you ask?"

"Because I'm a believer now."

The guard chuckled. "What's going on?"

David leaned up in his chair. He placed his coffee mug on the counter next to the gate controls. "Well, me and my wife bought this trailer. We started playing this spirit board in there and things began to happen. Unexplainable noises, shadows, and dozens of roaches that came from out of nowhere. My wife saw a real ghost outside the trailer not once, but twice. They stuck around long enough for her to paint them on a canvas."

"You know what they say about those spirit boards don't know?" The co-worker said.

"I do now. After the fact. But it was just innocent fun. I didn't believe the board could give us the right answers to our questions."

"Wait," the guard replied quickly, taking a step back. "You mean to tell me that the board you used gave you correct answers?"

"Yes. Many times. But we stopped playing it after hearing and seeing things we hadn't before."

"You didn't throw it away did you?"

"No. I wanted to. But I just took it back to my dad's place and put it back in his shed."

"Let me tell you something. I bought the old Richardson place off Highway 4 a couple of years ago. You know, the one with the loop-around driveway in the front? It has the columns along the front porch?"

"I think so," David said, still not sure.

"Well, me and my wife began hearing strange noises in the house about two weeks after moving in. We could hear faint voices. We couldn't make out what they were saying, but people were talking for sure. We never could tell what part of the house it was coming from either. When we got home from work, things would be on the floor broken. We had a lamp break; some on Martha's dishes were on the floor broken; things that couldn't be explained. So, I got in touch with this paranormal investigation team out of Baton Rouge. They came over and tested that house up and down. And you know what they found?"

"Ghosts?" David responded.

"Yes, and plenty of them. I told my wife we're not living with dead people. So, we moved out. Believe me, it isn't worth it."

"This paranormal team. How'd you get in touch with them?"

"I may still have their business card on me." The man pulled out a stack of cards from his wallet and began fishing through them. He took one out of the stack. "Here's their number. Just call them up and explain what your problem is. Then you'll make an appointment for them to come out. They usually come out within the next two days. It's two of them and they know what they're doing. They got all this equipment and testers for tracking down the ghosts. It's interesting to watch them work."

David looked down at the card. "I'll give them a call."

ℓ

After David returned home that day, he took a shower and slept 'til 3 that afternoon. He decided to wait until Erica returned home from that evening before picking up Billy from Pam's. Pam has been watching Billy ever since David and Erica left him there the morning before going to see the previous owners. David knew that Erica was missing him and would want to get him as soon as she got home. David was missing him very much too.

After waking up around 3:30, David grabbed his wallet from the top of the drawer. He pulled out the business card that his co-worker had given him. He looked at the number for a second, then picked up the phone and called them. A young girl answered the phone by the name of Sierra. She asked David some typical questions about their experiences in the house. He didn't mention the spirit board though. After a five-minute question and answer session, an appointment was made for the team to come over the next day and test the house. The appointment was made around seven. Sierra explained that ghosts are more active at nightfall.

A little after four, Erica walks in, slamming the door behind her.

"What's the matter sweetie?" David asked.

"I just got back from Pam's and she and Billy are not there," Erica replied.

"Well, don't worry," David said, trying to calm her. "Let me call Rich and see what's up. Maybe he knows where they are."

David calls his brother at work. Richard picks up the phone. "Hello?"

"Hey Rich, this is David. Do you know where Pam may be at with Billy? Erica just got back from your place and they're not there."

"I don't know bro. She did say something about going to the store before I left this morning. Maybe she took him shopping with her."

"You get off in about thirty minutes, right?"

"Yeah. I'll call you when I get home. She may be home by then too. I'll call you back."

"Thanks Rich. Erica wanted to pick up Billy."

"I'll let you know something bro."

David hung up the phone. "He thinks maybe she's at the store sweetie. Rich is going to call me back here soon. Why don't you take a nice hot shower and when you get out, we can go over and get him."

"Ok," Erica said, still upset. "But first let me call my sister."

David handed her the phone. Erica walks into the bedroom and shuts the door. David found that a little strange. Usually, Erica would talk to her sister right in front of him.

"Hi sis. It's Erica."

"Oh hi," Amanda replied, hesitant. "Is everything ok?"

"Well, there's been a lot going on here lately. I don't want to get into it right now. I was wondering how Stephen is doing?"

Amanda was silent for a moment. "Stephen?"

"Well, the board gave him a date on when he was going to die."

Amanda started to laugh. "Oh, yea but that was a lie. The date was yesterday. He's fine. He's sitting here on the couch."

"Thank God," Erica replied with relief.

"Are you ok sis?"

"Yea I'm fine. I've just had a long day at work I guess."

"Go take a nice hot bubble bath. Just sit in the hot water and let it relax your muscles. You'll feel better, I promise."

"Yea you're right. David just said about the same thing. Amanda, I also wanted to apologize for my behavior towards you."

"Don't worry Erica," Amanda replied. "I understand where you were coming from. We should've never done that. I'm the one who is sorry we broke in and played with that board. I'm hoping you've ditched that board by now."

"Yes. We took it back to where David found it. But, it's still crazy here."

"If there's anything I can do, just let me know."

"Thanks sis. I'll let you go. Talk to you later."

Erica opened the bedroom door and walked into the living room, placing the phone on the end table next to David. David didn't question her about the conversation she had with Amanda. He could tell she had a long day and now Pam and Billy are nowhere to be found. He wasn't going to make it worse by asking her about the conversation. If Erica wanted him to know, she would tell him.

"I'm going to shower now," Erica said, slipping off her shoes. "I might take a bubble bath."

David looked into Erica's eyes. "Come here. Sit in my lap for a second."

Erica did, putting her arm around his neck for support. David began rubbing Erica's legs. Then he kissed her. "How about tonight, I give you a foot massage."

Erica's eyes lit up. "Wow. You haven't given me one of those since our honeymoon. What's the occasion?"

David smiled. "I just want to. Go take your bubble bath, then we'll go get Billy. After dinner, we'll sit down and watch a movie while I give you a foot massage. How's that sound. We'll have a relaxing evening. How's that sound?"

"That sounds good," Erica said, leaning forward to kiss him again. "And normal," she added with a smile.

Erica took a nice hot bubble bath. She was listening for the phone to ring, but never heard it. Or maybe Richard called while she was running the water. After getting out, she opened the bathroom door with a towel around her and shouted down the hallway to David. "Heard anything yet?"

"No, not yet," David replied.

"Can you call him back? It's been nearly an hour."

Just then the phone rang.

David picked up. "Hello?"

"Hey bro," Richard said, "I just got home and Pam's not here."

"Where do you think she could be Rich? Surely she's not at the store this long."

"Well, she didn't go to the store bro. The grocery list is still laying here on the counter."

David's thoughts began racing. "Rich, we're getting worried. You have no idea where she might be?"

"Y'all not the only ones worried. When Pam goes somewhere, she always calls me to let me know, or she leaves a little note on the countertop. Give me a few minutes ok. Let me look around and see what I…"

"Rich? What is it?"

"It's a letter. She left it on our bed. It says:
Dear Richard, I'm sorry for not being able to give you a child of your own. You deserve so much more than what I can provide. I've messed up our lives and there's no way I can make it better. I only hope you can forgive me. The only child I'll ever have is little Billy. He's with me. I fear that his life is in danger so long as he's living in that haunted trailer. He's in good hands now. In time, Erica will understand why I'm doing this. She knows I love little Billy very much and would do anything to make sure he's safe from those demons. Again, I'm sorry for everything. Don't try to look for me. I will talk to you again, but I don't know when. Pam"

David stood up from his chair. "Rich…you didn't tell her."

"I'm sorry bro. I…"

"Where could she be? She's got our boy."

Erica rushed into the living room, hearing David. "What? Where are they?"

"Bro, I wish I knew but I…wait."

"What is it Rich? Do you know where they are?"

"Our camp on the lake…the keys to the camper are missing."

"We'll follow you down there."

"Ok, but let's not go in storming the place. According to this letter, she's unstable."

"And she's got our son," David said. "His life is in danger."

19

"Faster!" Erica shouted as they stormed down the long stretch of highway 9. "I hope he's ok."

"I'm sure he's fine," David replied, trying to ease her worries. "Before you know it, you'll be holding him tightly in your arms again."

Richard wasn't far behind them. He was driving as fast as he could, exceeding the speed limit without hooking a cop on his tail. But then, he thought, maybe it wouldn't be a bad idea to get the cops involved. Hopefully, Pam hasn't reached the point of no return. He was kicking himself for not telling her about his doctor visit. *If only I'd told her about it, we wouldn't be in this mess.*

"This was supposed to be a relaxing evening for us," Erica said. "Pam won't be babysitting Billy after this fiasco."

"I'm sorry things turned out like this," David said, "but we must focus on getting Billy back and making sure that Pam will be safe."

"I should've seen this coming," Erica said. "Every time Pam would talk about her pregnancy issue, she would always bring up the fact that she's only cared for Billy."

"You couldn't predict this sweetie. There was no way of knowing that Pam was becoming unstable."

"You know, I called her this morning to tell her that I would be picking up Billy as soon as I got off work. That's when she started asking me questions about what we found out from the previous owners of the trailer. I told her some things I shouldn't have, but I figured what's the harm. Now I know. We should've picked him up as soon as we got back from seeing Rebecca."

"You shouldn't beat yourself up for that. Like you said, you didn't see any harm in it."

Erica was silent. She ran her fingers through her hair, hoping they would get to the campsite quickly. "I just want Billy back," Erica finally said. "I miss him."

David turned to Erica and took her hand, holding it gently. "I miss him too."

Richard and Pam purchased a half-acre of land right on the lake just several months ago. They both enjoyed fishing and camping, so it was like a gift for them. Richard had bought a camper trailer from a buddy of his to set down on their small piece of land, near the edge of the lake. Richard and Pam would spend some weekends down there, enjoying the peacefulness and all the fishing they could do.

As David crossed the bridge over the lake, they slowed down to turn off the first road on the right. David and Erica had only been here once – a week after Richard and Pam bought the place. Erica looked out on the lake. Cypress trees dominated the waters of the lake. Moss and seaweed were visible at the surface level. The narrow, bumpy dirt road led them straight to Richard and Pam's camp. As they drove up to the camper trailer, they noticed Pam's car parked beside it.

"Rich was right," David said, relieved. "She's here."

Richard drove up just seconds later, parking behind David. He saw David and Erica get out of the truck. "Bro, wait! Let me handle this."

David turned to his brother. He motioned Erica to stop. "Go ahead Rich," he said.

Richard approached the trailer, slowly. Just then, Pam screamed out from the kitchen window. "Don't come any closer! None of you!"

"Pam," Richard shouted, "I just want to talk to you. Please honey."

"No!" Pam cried out. "I told you not to follow me. You never listen to me."

"Look honey," Richard said, "just give Billy back to David and Erica and then you and I will sit down and talk ok?"

"No!" Pam shouted. "If I let Billy go back to that trailer he'll be in danger. I can't let that happen."

Erica shook her head. "I can't believe her," she said quietly to David.

"Besides," Pam continued, "he's happy with me. I can take good care of him."

Richard didn't know how to respond. He looked back at Erica.

"Is she crazy?" Erica said. "I want my son back."

"Pam," Richard said, "listen to me honey. It's not your fault that we can't get pregnant."

"Yes it is," Pam shouted. "I'm not capable of having a child."

"You don't know that honey," Richard said.

"I do. The board said it was my fault."

Richard turned to David. David was just as shocked to hear it.

"Honey," Richard said. "When did the board tell you this?"

Pam was silent for a moment, then she spoke. "Yesterday."

Richard's eyes widened. "Yesterday? Did you play that board yesterday?"

"Yes," Pam replied. "I invited Janine over to play with me. I asked the board if I was ever going to get pregnant and it said no. It also said that I wasn't capable of having a child."

Richard stretched over the deck railing, trying to see through the kitchen window. He could see Pam pacing back and forth with Billy in her arms. He looked out at David who was waiting for a solution. Richard thought about kicking the door in when Pam spoke again.

"The board also predicted that Billy would be in danger."

"Danger?" Richard asked. "What are you talking about?"

"I asked the board if Billy would ever be in danger while living in that trailer and the board said yes."

Erica began approaching the trailer. "That's it. I've heard enough."

David tried to hold Erica back, but she broke free of his grip.

Richard stood in front of the door. "I can't let you go in there Erica," Richard said.

"Either you go in and bring me my son or I'll do it myself," Erica said sternly.

Richard knew she meant it. He could tell that she was scared for her son and that she wanted this to be over.

"Let me go in," Richard said.

Richard entered the trailer. Pam scurried to the bedroom and slammed the door.

"I told you not to come in," Pam said.

David and Erica could hear her from outside. They traded worried looks as they waited for Richard to bring Billy to them.

"Honey," Richard said in a calm voice, "the board is wrong."

"No it's not," Pam replied. "That board has never been wrong."

Richard stood next to the bedroom door. "I have proof that the board is wrong."

Pam didn't respond.

Richard pulled out a piece of paper from his pocket. He unfolds it, waiting for Pam to say something.

Pam had heard Richard unfolding the paper. "What kind of proof?"

"I have it in my hand right now," Richard said, still hating to tell his wife about his condition. "Open the door and I'll show it to you."

Pam hesitated. "This is a setup," she shouted. "You're just trying to get me to open this door so you can grab little Billy."

"No!" Richard shouted. "I have medical proof that it's my fault we're not getting pregnant."

Pam didn't respond.

"Please honey, just open the door. Please."

Just then, the door opened slowly. Pam stepped out with Billy in her arms. "Where's this proof?"

Richard gave the paper to Pam. She put Billy down but was still holding his hand as she read the paper.

"That's a medical report," Richard said, "stating that my sperm count is too low. There's a small chance of me getting you pregnant."

After reading the paper, Pam looked up at Richard, a tear leaving her eye. She noticed the date on the paper. "Why didn't you tell me this before?"

Richard sighed. "I was ashamed of myself. I was afraid you'd think of me as less of a man. I didn't want you to see me in that way."

"You shouldn't think that." Pam was silent for a moment as she looked into Richard's eyes. "You're my husband. I love you…no matter what."

Richard began to smile. "I'm sorry for not telling you about this sooner."

Pam smiled back. "Thanks for telling me now."

Richard and Pam shared a kiss, while Pam continued holding onto Billy. David and Erica were wondering what was going on.

"You think I should go in?" Erica asked.

"Just give them some time," David replied. "I don't hear any shouting."

Just then, Pam walked out with Billy. Erica had to catch her breath. Billy went running to his mom who picked him up and squeezed on him. David smiled at the sight of his boy back with them. He noticed Richard walking out the door, stuffing a piece of paper in his pocket.

"Don't worry," Pam said. "Little Billy is fine. I'm just scared that something will happen to him if he keeps living in that trailer."

"Don't worry about that Pam," David said. "I called a paranormal team to come out and take care of it for us."

Erica looked at David, surprised. "I didn't know you called a paranormal team."

"I haven't had a chance to tell you," David replied. "I'll fill you in on the drive home."

Pam approached David and Erica, who was still holding onto Billy for dear life.

"I'm sorry," Pam said. "I didn't mean for all this to happen."

"It's my fault honey," Richard said. "I should've told you about this earlier."

Richard looked at David. David smiled at his brother as to say everything will be ok. Without saying a word to Richard or Pam, Erica took Billy back to the truck.

"She's still shaken up from all this," David said. "She'll be fine."

"Honey, "Richard said, "would you mind waiting for me back inside the trailer. I need to talk with my bro here for a second."

"Sure," Pam said, walking slowly back to the trailer.

"I'm glad you finally told Pam everything," David said.

"I'm sorry that I didn't tell her earlier," Richard said. "All this wouldn't have happened."

"The important thing is that everyone is okay."

"Yea, but just to be on the safe side, I think you and Erica should get another babysitter. Pam needs some time alone right now. She needs me to help her through this."

"I agree," David said. "If you need me for anything, let me know."

"Thanks David," Richard said, placing his hand on David's shoulder. "Thanks for everything."

"Hey, that's what brothers are for." David began to make his way towards the truck.

Richard began thinking about what Pam said earlier. "Hey, you know something?" Richard said to David.

David turned around. "What's that?"

"Now that Pam has played the board in our trailer, does that mean it's haunted too?"

David paused for a second, and then a smile came across his face. "Naw. When the ghosts get one look at you, they'll high-tail it out of there."

Richard shook his head. "Very funny bro. Very funny."

"I'm just joking Rich. I wouldn't worry about it if I was you."

"Yeah you're right. It couldn't be as bad as what you got it."

"That's true. Speaking of which, I've got a date with the devil."

"That's no way to talk about Erica like that."

"No. I am talking about our confrontation with the demon in our house. Supposedly his name is Kasdeya."

"What kind of name is that?"

"Enough that it has our attention," David replied.

20

David could tell that the paranormal team had arrived at their house the next day. They were driving a black van with the words "Paranormal Investigators of LA" across the side of the van. David smiled at the thought of two bozos coming in, tripping over their equipment, running from one end of the trailer to the next screaming "ghosts!". He's hoping to get a professional team to tell him exactly what he and Erica are dealing with – not a sideshow. As he peeked out the window, he saw a young man step out of the van and a young woman get out from the other side. The man opened the back of the van, while the woman headed for the front door.

"Are you David Chandler?" the woman asked.

"That's me," David replied.

"Good evening. My name is Sierra. Ashton is gathering our equipment. We are the Paranormal Investigators you requested."

"Please come in," David said.

"Thank you," Sierra replied, making her way in.

Sierra began her walk through the trailer, observing, jotting down notes on her clipboard. Her blonde hair tied in a long ponytail, wearing black and white sneakers, and cargo pants David got the impression she was unprofessional; yet, her walkthrough and observations showed she's been doing this work for years. He was uncertain about his decision to bring them in at this point. She exchanged small chit chat with David while gathering her notes. It was small talk about him and his family. No talk about ghosts, yet.

Ashton was grabbing several items from the van and placing them in a bag when he noticed Arthur Rasberry peeking through the shrubs. From the corner of his eye, he stared at the old man for a minute, then went back to filling the bag. Arthur put on his glasses to read the letters on the van. "So, David finally decided to get help," he thought to himself. Ashton began to work faster in collecting the things he needed for the investigation. Arthur was making him uncomfortable.

When Ashton walked through the door with his bag around his shoulder and a tripod in his right hand, Sierra introduced him to David. Ashton dropped his bag on the floor.

"It's a pleasure to meet you David," Ashton said, extending his hand. Ashton wore black-framed glasses, his brown hair grown out over his ears, wearing a t-shirt and jeans.

"It's my pleasure," David replied. "I'm very glad and relieved that you could make it here tonight. I'm ready to get to the bottom of this ghost fiasco once and for all."

"Well that's why we're here," Sierra said. "Now why don't we sit over here on the couch while Ashton gets things setup. I'd like for you to tell me from the beginning what's been going on in here."

"Sounds good," David said. He was hoping that Erica would get back with Billy soon. She had dropped off Billy at her mom's before going to work this morning. She told David that she would pick Billy up before coming home. He wanted to give Erica a chance to tell her side of the story as well. She had seen and heard much more than he had.

David watched as Ashton placed the tripod in the corner of the living room, facing the hallway. He then attached a camera to it. He did the same thing in the kitchen, facing the camera at the bedroom entrance. Ashton couldn't help but step on roaches as he worked.

"You have a serious roach problem David," Ashton said.

"Tell me about it," David replied. "We started having that problem around the time we started hearing things."

"Ok," Sierra said, "I want you to start at the beginning. Tell me what the first thing you saw or heard and go from there. I need to know the location of the incidents and a good guess of the time it happened. That's very important. I'll create a timeline of the events as you tell it. Whenever you're ready."

David paused for a minute. "You want me to start at the time we played the spirit board?"

Sierra looked up at Ashton, who stopped working. "A spirit board was played inside this trailer?" Sierra asked with a stern voice.

"Yes," David said. "That's when things started happening."

Sierra looked away in surprise. "Why didn't you mention the spirit board over the phone yesterday?" Sierra asked.

"I don't know," David replied. "I didn't get the chance. Does it matter? The house is still haunted."

"Spirit boards are used to conjure up spirits," Ashton remarked. "They are drawn to things such as spirit boards."

"Still," David said, getting upset. "Does it matter?"

"It certainly adds a piece to the puzzle," Sierra said, looking at Ashton. "We will still conduct our investigations, but you may not like what we find."

David looked away from Sierra. "What is that supposed to mean?"

"We've done investigations involving spirit boards before," Ashton said. "And the outcomes weren't for the faint at heart. If our investigation turns out the way I'm expecting, you may want to find another place to live."

"That's ridiculous," David said. "Let's just do the investigation and see what happens, ok? There's no sense in coming to a conclusion right now."

"Ok," Sierra said. "Then start at the spirit board. Leave nothing out. Since your wife isn't here, you will need to include what she saw and heard as well."

David and Sierra sat on the couch, as David rehashed everything that has happened to him and Erica over the last two months. He told Sierra about their experiences with the spirit board, Erica seeing the woman and child, Mr. Rasberry becoming ill inside their home, their roach problem, the sounds heard at night, the feeling of someone watching them and the letters were drawn on the mirror. What he didn't talk about was the board's predictions regarding Pam and how she became unstable with Billy. He also didn't mention Mr. Rasberry or his dad playing the board.

After the interview was over, Sierra and Ashton walked around the house, with a camera and tape recorder. As they were working, Erica walked in with Billy.

David approached them. "Hey sweetie," David said, hugging Billy. "How was your day?"

"It was good," Erica replied, looking at the investigators in the other room. "How're things around here?"

"I guess we'll know in a few minutes. I've already given them the rundown on what's been going on around here."

"What are they doing exactly?" Erica asked, trying to make sense of their work.

"They're checking for negative energy. These cameras are set up to capture a spirit moving around the house."

"It's strange."

"I know."

Just then, Sierra walked into the living room. "Are you Erica?"

"Yes," Erica said.

"I'm Sierra and that's Ashton in your son's bedroom. We're the paranormal investigators. How are you?"

"I'm fine," Erica said. "I hope y'all can do something about these ghosts in here."

"We're going to try," Sierra said, not sounding too convincing.

"Ok," Ashton said, walking out of Billy's bedroom, "we're done with our preliminary investigations. Tonight, we'll have these three cameras rolling and hopefully we'll pick something up."

"So these cameras will be running all night?" David asked.

"Yes," Sierra said. "You said you work tonight, right?"

"Well yes," David replied, "but Erica and Billy will be here."

"It would be better if no one was in the trailer tonight," Ashton said. "Is there somewhere you and Billy can go?"

"Well," Erica said, trying to think, "I guess we could stay with my mom tonight."

"Sweetie, are you sure?" David asked.

"Yeah," Erica replied. "It shouldn't be a problem. I just need to grab some things first."

"Ok," Sierra said. "When everyone is ready to leave, we'll flip on the cameras and they will record the next nine hours. Tomorrow morning, we'll come back for the cameras and test them out. Ashton will be running this EVP that we just recorded through our computer enhancement software. There's something on it."

"What's an EVP?" Erica asked.

"It stands for Electronic Voice Phenomena," Sierra said. "It is a recording of voices on audiotape from unknown sources. The tape picks up what we cannot naturally hear. It's a little jumbled up right now, but we'll be able to make it audible"

"Ok," David said. "Sounds good."

"Great," Sierra said. "Ashton and I will go back to the van to get a few more things. We'll wait until you're ready to leave."

Erica began packing for her overnight stay with her mom. She packed some extra clothes for work in the morning as well as some extra clothes for Billy. David got ready for work.

Ashton placed the audio recorder in the back of the van. He closed the back door of the van and looked over towards the shrubs. He thought he saw the old man again, but he was only imagining. Sierra joined Ashton behind the van, putting her hands around his waist and kissing him on his lips.

"I think this job will put us on the map," Sierra said.

"I agree," Ashton replied. "There's some serious negative energy inside that trailer; the most I've ever detected. And that EVP is probably our best one yet."

"And when we catch something on those cameras, we'll be rich and famous," Sierra said.

"I like the sound of that," Ashton replied.

The two embraced in another kiss. Then, Ashton stopped, looking over at the shrubs again. "Damn it."

"What is it?" Sierra asked, looking towards the shrubs.

"I keep thinking that an old man is looking at us through those shrubs."

"You're jumpy," Sierra noticed. "Since when are you afraid of an old man."

"I'm not afraid," Ashton replied, looking back at the shrubs again.

"You've crossed paths with a real ghost before," Sierra said. "Now you're getting jumpy about an old man?"

"Can we just forget it?" Ashton said, taking her hand and kissing it.

Just then, they heard the front door of the trailer open. "Ashton? Sierra?" David called out. "We're leaving."

Sierra turned to Ashton. "It's showtime," she said with a devilish smile.

21

David and Erica were watching TV when Ashton and Sierra knocked on the door the next evening.

"Come in," David said, stepping aside. "I hope you have something to tell us."

Sierra and Ashton didn't say anything. Just concern looks on their faces. As they entered the living room, Ashton pulled out the tape recorder from his bag.

Sierra smiled at Erica. "How are you?"

"I'm good," Erica replied. "Unless you have bad news to tell us."

Ashton cut in. "We analyzed this recording every which way possible. It was one of the most difficult recordings we've dealt with."

"Why is that?" Erica asked.

"We're uncertain," Ashton replied. "It begins as a normal recording, but then there's so much going on that I wasn't sure if it was static or voices. After analyzing it, we could tell what it was."

David and Erica stared at Ashton, waiting for the answer.

"Voices," Ashton said. "There are many of them."

"Ok," David said, "I'm not sure what you're telling me here."

Sierra replied, "Well, for one thing, your house is haunted. Secondly, there's more than one entity living here. Ashton, play the tape for them."

Ashton placed the tape in the audio player. "This message was repeated throughout the tape. This is as clear as I could get it."

David and Erica could hear static, followed by sharp interruptions. Then, they heard the message. "*…get out…this place…belongs to us…leave now.*"

"That message was repeated countless times throughout the recording," Sierra said. "You'll hear it again within the next twenty minutes."

"What the hell does that mean?" David asked.

"Well," Ashton said, "if I was to take a guess, I'd say that the ghost has claimed your house as its own. And you and your family are trespassing."

"This is unbelievable," David said, shaking his head in frustration.

Sierra replied, "Things of the supernatural usually are. But it doesn't mean that it isn't real or that this threat shouldn't be taken lightly."

"So," David replied, "you want us to just pack up and move somewhere else? It's not going to happen. We're staying right here."

"There were other voices on this recording," Ashton said. "A voice that said you were in danger."

Erica replied, "Who's in danger?"

"It didn't say," Ashton replied. "I assumed it meant all of you."

"Can I have a copy of that recording," David asked. "I want to listen to it."

"This is your copy," Ashton said, handing the audiotape to David.

Erica sat in shock. "I don't know about all this. The whole thing is all starting to freak me out."

Sierra walked up closer to them. "We don't usually get to investigate a house with so much activity going on. You haven't seen what our cameras picked up yet."

"My God!" David said. "I was so wrapped up in the audiotape that I completely forgot about the cameras. What did you pick up?"

Sierra turned to Erica. "Where is your son?" Sierra asked.

"He's in his room playing," Erica said. "Why?"

"I don't want him seeing what we discovered on these cameras," Sierra replied. "It just wouldn't be good for him to see this."

"You're scaring the crap out of me," Erica said. "I'm not sure I want to see it now."

Ashton put the videotape inside their VCR and hit play. David and Erica sat back, waiting nervously at what the cameras picked up.

"This camera was placed behind the TV, facing the hallway," Ashton said, pointing down the hall. "As you can see in the left corner of the screen, the rocking chair."

"Yea," David said.

"Keep your eyes on it," Ashton said.

A few moments later, the chair began to rock, with no one in it. David and Erica were shocked, but not so frightened as they've seen that before. Then the chair stopped after a few minutes. The video produced some static, almost disappearing from the screen. Then, the transparent image of a man in uniform appeared on the screen. He was holding a shotgun in his hand. David stared stone cold at the video, unable to breathe. Erica placed her hand over her mouth, gazing at the sight of the ghost.

"That has to be Abbot Brown," Erica whispered.

"Yes…it is," David said.

They all watched as Abbot, holding a shotgun, walk down the hallway and into the back room. Then, a gunshot was heard.

"We've heard that before," Erica said. "During the night, we heard a baby cry and then the sound of the gun."

"That's called a death echo," Ashton said. "The victim lives out their death repeatedly. It can usually be heard but never seen. This is a rare event we're viewing here."

Sierra cut in. "Now look down the hallway. Keep your eye on that far back bedroom door."

After a moment, the door quickly slammed shut. David and Erica gasped for breath. Then they saw what looked like black and purple smoke floating in the air, making its way down the hallway, then disappearing.

"What the hell was that?" David asked.

"That's called an apparition," Ashton said. "And since the apparition was so visible, it's also very powerful."

"I have a good guess as to who that is," David said. "It's Kasdeya."

Sierra nodded. "Our thoughts exactly. Usually an apparition like that wouldn't be seen in human form until it possesses someone and uses their body as a medium."

Erica shook her head. "All this foreign talk of ghosts is driving me insane. I'm sorry. I don't understand what you just said."

"The only way for a ghost-like Kasdeya to manifest into a human form is to possess the body of another human and use their body as a vessel to perform physical actions."

Erica still had a glazed look in her eyes from all the ghost speak. "So, what you're saying is that for… Kasdeya… to walk this earth, he has to enter a living human?"

"Exactly," Sierra replied. "In most cases. It can be done in other ways, but it's not usually the case. That type of apparition isn't considered a ghost at all. It's a demon."

"Whoa," David said, shaking his head. "Slow down for a second. Now you're talking about demons. These are just ghosts that have entered our home because we played some stupid board game. We're not gonna blow this out of proportion here."

"That collection of smoke is an apparition," Ashton replied. "It should be taken seriously. Very seriously. There's no telling what that demon is capable of."

"Ashton's right," Sierra replied. "This demon is using Abbot Brown to replay a horrible event repeatedly. But this demon can be capable of much more."

David and Erica look back at the TV, watching the ghost of Abbot Brown walk down the hallway again, reliving the death of his son.

With everyone's back turned to the hallway as they watched the video, a shadowy figure appeared in the living room. Erica first noticed the shadow casting over the TV. She couldn't breathe. She couldn't move. She wanted to warn the others, but she was paralyzed.

"Mommy," Billy said. "That's the man I saw in my bedroom."

Everyone turned around to see little Billy pointing at the TV at the ghost of Abbot Brown, disappearing into the darkness of the hallway.

"Billy!" Erica shouted, trying to catch her breath. "You scared us! What are you doing up?"

"I couldn't sleep mommy," Billy said.

Sierra reached over and quickly turned the tape off.

David approached Billy. "Billy, are you sure that was the man you saw?" David asked.

"Yes daddy that was him. He was in my room watching me. The army man. He told me to go outside and bring wee jee back in."

"Oh God!" Erica gasped.

David turned to Erica, who was still breathing heavily. "Are you ok sweetie?"

Erica shot David a stare as to signify a definite no. "I'm just going to get Billy and me a glass of water."

Erica took Billy into the kitchen, stepping on roaches as they approached the fridge. David turned his attention to the investigators.

"I think that's all we can take today," David said.

Sierra came closer to David. In a low voice she said, "I would suggest getting in touch with a psychic, who can come in and cleanse the home. Here are a few good ones. You should compare psychics and see which one fits you the best. A good psychic will do a complete cleansing on this home. I highly suggest it."

"Thank you," David said. "I appreciate this."

Sierra stared at David. "Because I know you're not going to leave. Not yet anyway. This is the next best thing for you and your family."

David didn't respond.

"But don't expect a miracle," Sierra said, walking to the front door. "This home needs some serious help."

"Have a safe trip back," David said, opening the door.

As Ashton and Sierra made their way out the door, Sierra turned back to David. "I hope things work out for all of you. I've seen similar events like this become life-threatening for the owners. Your situation is the worst we've ever seen. I don't want that to happen to your family. I just hope that you'll take this seriously and make sure that they're safe."

David parted a smile. "I appreciate your concern. I do. You don't have to worry though. I love my family and I'll do everything in my power to make sure that they're safe. I would never put them in danger."

Ashton stood next to Sierra. "But isn't that what you're doing right now? By living in that trailer, you're all in danger."

David didn't respond. A grim look came across his face.

"Let's go Sierra," Ashton said, as he took her hand.

David watched them walk back to their van, then he closed the door. He had to be at work in one hour.

⌐

3:44 AM

Erica was asleep with Billy next to her in bed. She woke up suddenly, looking over at Billy who was sound asleep. Then, she heard voices.

Listening closely, it sounded like chants. She got out of bed and walked into the kitchen. She could still hear the voices coming from the bedroom on the other side of the trailer. As she walked into the living room, she looked at the rocking chair that was still. The voices began to faint as she got closer to the bedroom. As she entered the hallway, she felt chill bumps all over her body. She was frightened but very curious. As she approached the bedroom door, the voices stopped. She opened the door and not surprisingly there was nothing there.

Just then, the door to her bedroom slammed shut. Erica looked down the hallway and she heard it lock. "Billy?" Erica shouted. She rushed to the bedroom door, but she couldn't open it. "Billy, can you hear me? Open the door Billy." Erica didn't hear Billy respond. Was he in deep sleep? She tried breaking the door down, worried that something was in the room with Billy. She began to panic, ramming her shoulder into the door that wouldn't budge. Still crying out to her son. "Billy!" Was Billy even alive she thought? So much was running through her head. Then at that moment, Billy opened the door and Erica nearly fell trying to get in. "Billy are you ok?" Erica shouted, hugging Billy tightly.

"Yes mommy," Billy replied. "You scared me."

"I'm sorry sweetie. Mommy didn't mean to."

"What were you doing?" Billy asked innocently.

Erica tried to make up a story. "I…I went to get some water. That's all. I accidentally locked myself out." Erica tried laughing it off for Billy's sake. "I'm sorry I scared you."

Billy stood there rubbing his eyes.

"Come on," Erica said, looking around the room. "Let's get back in bed and try to get some sleep."

For the next thirty minutes, Erica laid in bed, looking over Billy who was fast asleep. She could feel the presence of someone in the room with them. An evil presence. She felt like it was waiting for her to fall asleep so it could kill her. She thought it was strange, especially when according to the board's prediction, she only had four days left.

22

David couldn't sleep the next morning after Erica told him about what happened to her and Billy. After Erica left for work with Billy, David took a quick shower and prepared for his trip to visit the psychic in person. He was determined to stop these ghosts from harming his family. The long stretch of highway after passing through Winnfield became tiring for David. He was not much of a traveler. He even dreaded to drive thirty minutes into the next biggest city, north of Jonesboro. Driving south from Jonesboro to Alexandria was even worse. A long stretch of highway and nothing but forest on both sides of the road.

After reaching Alexandria two hours later, David stopped at a convenience store and pulled out his map and the psychic's address. He bought a cookie and a soda before getting back on the road. Driving into the old part of Alexandria, he noticed it looked a lot like Jonesboro's main street district. As he slowly made his way into town, he spotted the psychic's shop. David pulled alongside the road and as he approached the shop, it said "Kristin's Psychic Reading".

David took a long deep breath before exiting his truck. David is as skeptical as they come on the abilities of a psychic. He grew up in a Baptist church in a southern town. He's naturally dubious of anything that entails a darkened room, crystal balls, and the occult. He peered through the glass windows of the shop, noticing odd items pertaining to the other world. David envisioned a blowsy woman with black ringlets and big hoop earrings, walking through beaded curtains who would conjure answers out of a crystal ball. "This is ridiculous," he thought.

David stepped through the door as a little bell rang out loud. "I'll be with you in a moment," a woman's voice called out from the back. David had never been in a psychic's shop before, nor did he ever have any reason to. He didn't believe in ghosts or talking to the dead before using the spirit board. The shop was lightly dimmed throughout. It had an unusual smell to it. A mixture of an old shop with the essence of the psychic world he assumed. He noticed glass jars with unusual things in them, a big wooden wheel with different objects of the earth on it, and then in the corner of the room was a spirit board. David's eyes widened. It wasn't like the spirit board he and Erica were using. It looked older, with octagon corners.

Just then, a woman stepped out from the back room. "I'm sorry about that," the woman said. "My name is Kristin."

David looked at her surprisingly. She was nothing like he envisioned. Kristin was like any housewife that you would pass on the street. Her fashion was contemporary, wearing a classic V-neck t-shirt over faded jeans. He noticed a ring on each finger. Kristin was a heavy-set woman with dark skin and long, dark, wavy hair. She looked to be in her late 40's.

"My name is David Chandler. "I need your help."

"Yes," Kristin replied. "Follow me." She reentered the back room and David followed her.

They sat at a table that was set up for card reading it seemed. The thick, round wooden table had a spiritual engraving across it. Kristin noticed David trying to make sense of it.

"It's called a devil's trap," she said with a smile.

"What the hell does it mean?" David asked.

"It keeps demons and spirits from entering while I'm conducting a reading on someone. I don't need that negative energy coming into my reading, so this protects it."

"Interesting," David said.

Kristin stared at David as if she was trying to read his mind. David just stared back.

"You're in some trouble," Kristin finally said. "You and your family."

"You're a psychic," David said. "You should know why I'm here."

"Well, naturally I can pick up on nearly everyone who comes through that door. About ninety percent of the time. The other ten percent usually have a certain type of psychic ability that hinders me from seeing the whole picture. You have that rare type of ability. Even so, I can sense that your family is in trouble, and your home is in danger."

David stared in surprise. "That's a good start."

"That's all I'm able to pick up at this point."

"Wait," David said. "Are you saying you can't fully read me because I'm a psychic?"

"Not exactly. You may have psychic abilities, but that doesn't mean you're a psychic. And since I'm a psychic, then it's sometimes hard for me to read another's thoughts. It's like an interference. Whether you decide to develop your abilities further is completely up to you."

"You're not the first person to tell me about my so-called psychic powers," David said.

"Would you like to learn more about it?" Kristin asked.

"No," David replied. "I didn't come here to talk about this. I came here because I feel that my family is in danger."

"Then please tell me what's going on," Kristin said, her full attention at David.

David collected his thoughts as best he could. "Well, me and my wife moved into a trailer house a few months ago. Everything seemed fine the first couple of weeks we were there, until myself, my wife, my brother, and his wife played this spirit board together one evening. After that, we began experiencing things like doors shutting, a presence in the room, things falling to the floor, voices in another room, and we have roaches like I've never seen. They are worse at night. Hundreds of them it seems. I had an exterminator come by and he said we have the cleanest trailer he's ever seen. My wife has seen ghosts of a woman and child who turned out to be the late wife and great-granddaughter of our neighbor next door. My wife and I have heard a ghost shoot a crying baby in the middle of the night. That freaked us out like you wouldn't believe. My wife and I even located the previous owner and she told us that her brother-in-law killed his wife and child, and then shot himself in the head in that trailer. We think he's haunting the place. But there's also another ghost or demon or whatever you call it haunting the place as well. And that's the thing I'm worried about the most. I have this feeling that that apparition, which we're calling Kasdeya, is the biggest threat to my family."

"You have a feeling?" Kristin asked.

"Yeah," David replied.

"Your psychic abilities are telling you that this Kasdeya demon is the main threat. You should go with your gut feeling on this and anything else that you feel strongly about. That's for future reference."

"Look Kristin," David said, nearly cutting her off, "this sounds like you're giving me psychic lessons here. I want your help in dealing with my house."

"I can help you David," Kristin said calmly. "Is this your first experience with a spirit board?"

"Yes," David said. "And it'll be my last."

"Do you know how old the board is?"

"It was manufactured in the 1950s."

"Then it's a seasoned board."

"Seasoned?"

"It's very active. It can move on its own or at least with only one person playing it. There's a way to keep the spirits from escaping by sprinkling silver on top of the board. It will keep away the bad spirits and allow you to have a satisfying experience without worrying about what might come through."

"Forget it," David said. "There won't be a next time. I put the board back where I found it. It can sit there and rot for all I care."

"Well anyway," Kristin continued, "do you know what to expect from a psychic or exactly what we do?"

"Uh, no I don't," David said. "Never had a reason to need the help of a psychic before."

"Ok," Kristin replied, "let me go through it with you. Psychics attempt to facilitate communication with spirits who have a message to share with others. And believe me, every spirit has a message to share. My job is to listen to and reproduce their message back to you. I can relate conversations with spirit voices; go into a trance and speak without knowledge of what is being said; allow a spirit to enter my body and speak through it; take on the ailments of a spirit, feeling the same physical problems the person had before they died. I also can smell a spirit. I can receive taste impressions from a spirit. And I have the ability to know something without receiving it through normal or psychic senses. It is a feeling of just knowing. Even though I consider myself mostly psychic, I also consider myself about twenty percent intuitive, meaning I'm right without a shadow of a doubt twenty percent of the time."

"Overall," David said, "how accurate are you?"

"It depends," Kristin replied. "I will give you in-depth insight instead of generalities, provide information to overcome the negativity in your life and I'm focused and clean in my readings. I will not be negative or judgmental and I will not make decisions for you or tell you what to do. I will see and hear it as it is and simply report my findings back to you."

"I'll be honest," David said. "You sound like a good psychic to me, but what about others. How do I know they wouldn't be better? You need to understand that I need a good psychic here."

"You don't know. You can't just compare psychics to one another. We differ by race, religion, culture, and of course, experience. You look for a psychic who's lived on the block for too long. And I know I've been here just five years now, but I've been doing this kind of work for nearly thirty years. I discovered my psychic abilities when I was eleven. You look for a psychic with a foundation built on hard work, honesty, reputation, and years of experience."

Kristin slid a sheet of paper to David. "Here are my references. Feel free to call them anytime."

David began looking at the references.

"You know," Kristin continued, "as of today, I have about 1800 clients. I travel to places like Africa and Asia to see some of them. I use tarot cards, astrology to tell people's futures. I'm good at what I do. I take this seriously. I'm not truly in it for the money, although I must make a living somehow. I was born to do this kind of work and I've helped many people using my psychic abilities."

David thought for a minute. "How do I know you're not a fake?"

Kristin chuckled as she leaned up. "I can understand your concern David. Con artists of generations past and today have put a stigma on the business and damaged the reputation of psychics who truly have worked hard to master their craft and seek to make a difference with their gift. Call those references. All one hundred of them. I can assure you. I'm as legitimate as they come."

"So how can you help me?" David asked.

"I would come into your home and get a real sense of the environment, taking notice of all the energy, good and bad, that inhabits your home. I would perform a cleansing of your entire home. The cleansing will get rid of all the negative energy inside your home and bring it back to normal."

"When can you come over?"

"Well, I have an opening late tomorrow afternoon. I can be at your house at six. Is that ok?"

"That's fine," David said, knowing that he had very little options. "Let me give you the address."

⌒

Erica returned home that evening with Billy. She spent an hour with David as he told her about Kristin coming over to do a cleansing. Erica felt a little at ease now that her and David found a way to rid the house of the ghosts.

That night, while David was at work, Erica let Billy sleep with her again. She stayed awake in bed for about thirty minutes, waiting for a sound. She also couldn't get her mind off the terrible prediction of her death, which was now just three nights away. She wanted to tell David about it, but she was afraid he'd get mad again once he found out she played the board by herself. She didn't want to believe that the prediction was right, but it was eating her up inside – just like David and Amanda said it would. What gave her a glimpse of hope was the fact that Stephen's prediction wasn't true. She hoped for the same.

Just then, she heard the backdoor slam shut. She stopped breathing, trying to listen. She heard nothing. Erica turned over to check on Billy. As usual, he was asleep. Erica got out of bed and slowly walked into the kitchen. She noticed that the roaches were everywhere and there were twice as many. She made her way to the back door. It was unlocked. She could hear a voice inside her head telling her to open it. She was afraid to but opened it anyway. She looked out in the backyard. It was a cemetery. There were grave markers everywhere. She stepped down the stairs and began walking towards the cemetery.

A light wind blew against her nightgown as she brushed her hair away from her face, looking at the cemetery, perplexed. She noticed that there were no writings on the grave markers except one. A marker in the very back of the cemetery. She made her way towards it to read the writing. She was shocked to see her name on the marker. Under her name it said, "died from supernatural causes". She shook her head in disbelief. "This can't be. No. This isn't happening." Just then, a shadowy figure approached her from behind. She quickly turned to see Abbot Brown, staring at her with a look of murder in his eyes. "No!" Erica shouted. "Stay away from me. Stay away!"

She began running for her life, back towards the trailer. When she got to the door, it slammed shut and locked. She tried breaking in, but she was too weak. She turned around to see Abbot walking towards her with a shotgun in his hand; the very same gun he used to kill his family with; the very same gun he committed suicide with. She tried desperately to get in, but she couldn't. Abbot began loading the gun as he slowly made his way towards Erica. Then, she noticed in the window, the figure of a dark man. "I know who you are," Erica said. "Kasdeya!" she shouted.

Kasdeya had reclaimed his house as his own and he left Erica to die. "No!" she shouted. "Please help me! Help me! No!"

"Mommy, mommy, wake up!" Billy shouted, shaking his mom like he was erasing an etch-a-sketch board. "Wake up!"

"Billy," Erica said, realizing that she was having a nightmare.

"Are you ok mommy?"

Erica hugged him. "Yes sweetie. Mommy was only having a bad dream."

Erica held onto Billy as she tried to ease her mind of the terrible nightmare.

23

The next day, Erica took Billy over to her Mom's when it was time for Kristin to arrive for the cleansing. David waited for Kristin, hoping that this would end their battle against the spirits. When Erica returned home, she noticed a car in the driveway and assumed it was the psychic.

"Hi," Erica said, walking through the door.

"Kristin," David said, "this is my wife Erica."

"And very lovely indeed," Kristin replied. "David has spoken very highly of you. How are you dear?"

"I'm holding up," Erica said, smiling at David. "How are you?"

"Well," Kristin replied, "I'm already weak from all the negative energy in your home. You have so many entities in this house; it's hard for me to focus on one single energy. Honestly, I feel sick to my stomach. The negative energy in this home does not want me here and is threatening my life with sickness."

Erica looked at David, with a worried look on her face. David knew what Erica was thinking. Could Kristin maintain her strength to perform the cleansing?

"Ok," Kristin said, taking a seat, "let me go over what I'm about to do. This is called a cleansing. It is the removal of everything evil, particularly the negative energy that has consumed this house. Today, I will perform what is called a sage ceremony. Sage ceremonies have been used since ancient times as a ceremony of purification."

Kristin begins to pull out objects from her bag. "The chosen plant material is dried and tied into bundles with a cotton string like I have here. Bundles are wrapped as thick as a person's hand can hold. Four colors of string are combined to honor the four directions of travel. That is white for the North, yellow for the South, red for the East and black for the West. This hallowed rock is used as a natural container to hold the mixture as it burns. To fan the embers, I'll use a feather fan for effectiveness. To keep smudge burning, I'll use matches."

"Now," Kristin said as she stood up slowly, "allow me to cleanse your home. We have eliminated all objects that attract negative energy throughout this home, so we are now ready to proceed. Do nothing but wait for me to complete the entire ceremony. I will tell you when I'm done."

David and Erica nodded in agreement.

Kristin began by lighting a smudge stick and drew the smoke over her head, shoulders, and heart. This process cleanses the psychic before the ceremony. Kristin proceeded into the back room where Erica kept her oil paintings and equipment. Kristin placed a bag of sage in each of the four corners of the room. Then she began to talk to the negative energy. "You are in no harm. We ask that you leave this place in peace. Kindly seek the light and move on. This house is for the living, not the dead. We wish you to depart from this place quietly."

"What?" David whispers from the living room. "She's talking to it like its innocent or something."

"Shhh," Erica said.

Kristin walked into the other rooms of the house, performing the same ritual, placing sage bags in each corner of the rooms and lighting them, allowing the rooms to be filled with smoke. Then she would say her message. She opened all closet doors and all the drawers in the kitchen. At the end of the ceremony, Kristin once again cleansed herself by drawing her smudge stick over her head, shoulders, and heart. She looked at David and Erica. "It's all done," she whispered.

"You mean, that's it?" David asked, not sounding convinced. "The ghosts are gone?"

"It may not seem like I did anything," Kristin said, "but the sage ceremony brings an awareness of the sacred and should be performed with sensitivity and respect. The smoke traps all negative energies and entities and carries them away. And the message I continued saying throughout the ceremony represents a painless goodbye to the spirits who were dwelling in your home. I have no doubt that your home is now cleansed."

"But how can you be certain?" Erica asked.

"Well," Kristin said with a smile, "for one thing, I feel much better. No more sickness inside me."

David and Erica smiled at each other in relief, thinking that they had their home back.

"Now," Kristin said, "I will take the ashes and combine them in one hallow rock and return them to "Mother Earth", the base of a tree perhaps."

"We have an old oak tree out back," Erica said.

"That will do just fine," Kristin replied.

Kristin combined the ashes and began to walk towards the back door. "I thank you so much for allowing me to come into your home and perform this successful cleansing for you."

"Hey," David said, "it's our pleasure. We've been desperate to rid our home of these ghosts."

"I'll strongly advise," Kristin said, "don't allow anything negative into this home. I'm talking about that spirit board. I know you told me that you were done with it, but just making sure. That's nothing to play around with."

"Trust us," David said, "we've learned our lesson."

"Kristin," Erica said, "can I ask you a question about the board?"

"Certainly," Kristin replied. "What's on your mind?"

"Well, the board made some predictions when we were using it. We've had some of our questions answered correctly, some questions not so accurate. What's your opinion on the board's ability to predict future events?"

David stared at Erica, wondering if there was something more to her inquiry.

Kristin sighed. "The spirit board is a mystery, darling. Its purpose is to communicate to spirits; not to give you the winning numbers to the lottery."

Erica nodded. "I see. But it correctly answered questions that were very personal to me."

Kristin stared at Erica as if she knew what she was thinking. "I'm not one hundred percent on this response, but I strongly feel you have nothing to worry about honey."

Erica smiled, relieved. "Thank you."

David gave Erica a curious look.

Kristin was heading for the door when suddenly, she fell to the floor, dropping her bowl of ashes that spilled across the carpet.

"Kristin!" David shouted, reaching down to pick her up. "Are you ok?"

Kristin returned to her feet, holding her stomach. It triggered David's memory of the incident with Mr. Rasberry.

"It's back," Kristin said, coughing up blood.

Erica gasped. "Oh God!"

"The negative energy has returned in full force."

Erica began to panic. "I thought you said it was over."

Kristin was sweating heavily. She wiped her brow and limped into the living room. "The energy is in this room. I can't get a fix on it. There are too many. Ah, I feel so weak."

194 | DONNY STEPHENS

"Kristin, we need to get you to a doctor," David said. "Let's get out of here."

"No!" Kristin shouted, waving him away. "That's what they want. They want you out of this house! That's the message I'm receiving from them. They say this house is theirs. The energy is strong. Stronger than I've ever felt before."

"What do we do?" Erica cried out.

Kristin coughed up more blood as she stood straight up, determined to release the house of the demonic possession. She reached for her bowl of remaining ashes and cast them into the air. "Get out I command! I demand you leave this place! This house is for the living. Leave now!"

Suddenly, all the lights shut off. The mirror on the wall suddenly fogged up from the heat that had consumed the room. Letters began to appear on it, spelling out *"you invited us"*. Kristin limped over to the mirror to read the words. Then, the mirror cracked right down the middle and Kristin was pushed back onto the floor.

"Kristin!" David shouted as he and Erica rushed to her. David and Erica lifted Kristen and dragged her down the hallway while Kristin screamed out words in Latin that neither David nor Erica could understand. Erica opened the back door and dragged Kristin onto the deck to get her out of harm's way.

"Kristin, can you hear me?" Erica asked.

"Yes dear," she said. "I'm fine."

"We'll take you to the hospital," David said.

"No!" Kristin demanded. "I've never been to a hospital in my life and I don't plan on going now. Just listen to me, will you? You need more help than I can give."

"Like what? God himself?" David asked.

Kristin turned to David with a look of fear upon her face. "You need a priest. This house needs an Exorcism!"

24

David stormed inside the house once Kristin had recovered and was on her way back. David was furious that the cleansing didn't rid their house of the demon.

"I've had it!" David shouted. "This house belongs to us. Do you hear me, demons? This is our house and we're not going anywhere! You get that?"

"Calm down," Erica said. "This isn't making things any better."

"I don't care," David replied. "They need to know this. They need to know that this is our house and we're not gonna take it anymore."

"You're being ridiculous."

"I'm being ridiculous?" David asked, turning to Erica. "You should be as mad as I am about this. These spirits nearly killed Kristin back there. She'll never come around here again. And now I must call a priest to come over? The hell with that."

"You might as well do what she says. What do we have to lose? We're already up to our necks in this."

"No!" David shouted. "I refuse to call a priest. These demons need to understand that this is our house. Not theirs. It's time for them to leave."

David walked around the room, looking up towards the ceiling and banging on the walls as if he was trying to get the attention of the spirits.

"I don't think they hear you, honey," Erica said. "You're not exactly a psychic or a priest you know."

David stopped banging the walls and turned to Erica. "On the contrary. I've had two people tell me that I am a psychic."

"What?" Erica asked. "What are you talking about?"

"Remember when I told you I felt something that wasn't right about the trailer the first time I stepped through the front door? Well, Kristin seems to think that that was my psychic abilities informing me of the negative energy in the house. Mr. Rasberry said the same thing… in so many words."

"So, you're a psychic now?"

"Not exactly. I mean, according to Kristin, we all have psychic abilities. It's just that I've never paid attention to them before. I passed it off as gut feelings."

"I would say that's all it is honey."

"Kristin says otherwise."

"This is all becoming too much for me to deal with. These ghosts and the demon and now you're a psychic."

David was silent, trying to understand what Erica was saying.

"I'm going to my mom's. I'll be staying there for the night. Billy and I."

"What?"

"I'm not going to subject our son to all this. And frankly, I don't want to live in a haunted house anymore. I already asked momma. She said it's fine with her."

"I'm not going anywhere. I'm staying right here."

"Fine. Whatever. I'm just gonna grab some things and head over there."

"I can't believe this. You're gonna leave me here by myself?"

"You're leaving for work in the next three hours. What difference does it make?"

"You're running. That's what the spirits want. You heard Kristin. They want us out. I'm not giving up our house just because of these spirits or demons or whatever you call them. We paid for this house with our money that took a year to save. I'm not going anywhere."

Erica shook her head. "I'll be at my mom's if you need me. You have her number. It's on the fridge."

David didn't reply. After Erica left, David laid down on the bed to take an hour nap before heading to work.

᠊

The next morning, David returned home and as usual, he ate breakfast and took a shower. Before going to bed, he called Erica's mom to say hi to Billy. It was already a humid day with the temperature close to ninety degrees. David turned the air conditioner on, setting the thermostat to seventy-three. David was tired from the night before, so it didn't take him long to fall asleep.

᠊

12:14 PM

A bead of sweat ran down the side of David's face. He laid in bed, breathing heavily, trying to get air. It felt like the heat was pressing down on him and he couldn't move. It was as if he was trapped. Paralyzed from the neck down, his arms and legs were useless. His throat was collapsing. He was scared of dying from the heat that was bearing down on him with a compelling force. And he couldn't stop it. Then suddenly, he awoke. He was sweating very heavily; he couldn't move. He looked around the edge of the bed. The covers were tucked tightly under the mattress, keeping him from moving at all. David struggled to break free, pulling and tugging to loosen the covers. He noticed the bedroom door was closed and he didn't hear the air conditioner running. "What's going on here?" he shouted.

He finally broke free from the covers and jumped out of bed. The bedroom door was locked from the inside. "I never lock this door," he said. David walked into the kitchen with sweat dripping off him. He took a towel from the counter and wiped his face with it. He grabbed a glass of water to wet his throat. Walking over to the thermostat, he noticed it was shut off. "Damn it!" he shouted. "They're trying to kill me!"

꧁

That evening, Erica called David from her mom's. David told Erica what happened to him earlier that day.

"You mean you talked to a priest?" Erica said.

"Yes," David replied. "Father McKinley, a Catholic Priest from Winnfield. Kristin gave him a briefing on our situation. He should be here in about an hour."

"How did you get him to come over so quickly?" Erica asked.

"I told him that our lives were in danger. I told him about what happened to me earlier today. He's taking this seriously."

"What can he do?" Erica asked.

"He can perform an exorcism on this place. Send these damn demons packing. I want you and Billy to stay at your mom's until this is over ok? I'll call you when we're done."

"Be careful," Erica said after a long pause. "I love you."

"I will sweetie," David replied softly. "I love you too."

꧁

Father McKinley pulled up to the Chandler's home. Arthur Rasberry watched through the shrubs as the priest exited his car, staring hard at the trailer. Arthur watched as

McKinley slowly made his way to the front door. He noticed David open the door just before McKinley stepped up onto the deck. Arthur shook his head, concerned. "I don't have a good feeling about this."

"David, how are you?" McKinley asked.

"To be honest with you, I'm not sure," David replied, letting the priest step through the door.

Father McKinley took a deep breath. He walked down the hall, into the living room, and approached the kitchen. He turned back to David. "This house is filled with many spirits. Some very evil I can tell you."

"How do you know?" David asked.

"I sense it. I've done numerous exorcisms in many homes and this is one of the most powerful I've encountered. There's no doubt that you and your family are in danger here. But I could sense that from our phone conversation earlier and Kristin's briefing."

"Can you help us get our home back?" David asked sincerely.

McKinley sighed. Well, it's not going to be an easy task David." McKinley cleared his throat. "To be brutally honest with you, I wouldn't expect a complete removal."

"But you will try."

"I'm going to try my best," McKinley said as he opened his briefcase. He began taking out several items while pondering over the situation. "You mentioned over the phone that a spirit board was played inside this house."

"Yes," David replied. "That's when all this got started."

"Is the spirit board still here?"

"No. I took it back to my father's place. I put it back where I found it."

"Good. We don't need anything in this house that will have the potential of giving off negative energy."

"You don't have to worry about that. I'll never play a spirit board ever again."

The priest was silent for a few minutes. He cleared his throat again. "You know, ever since I've been practicing the rites of exorcism, I've come across some very good people who have gotten themselves in a very deep hole in which they were barely able to make it back out." He pushed his thin-framed glasses closer to his eyes and looked at David. "After hearing what you've told me about the experiences your family has dealt with in this home, I can't help but think that this is another good decent family who has gotten way above their heads just because they don't understand the teachings of the Lord."

"What are you saying?"

"Are you a Christian David?"

"Yes. I am. So is my family."

"Then perhaps you can explain to me how you ended up practicing occult inside your home."

"Why did we play with the spirit board? Because we didn't believe in it. It was just a game to us, not a practice of the occult. We didn't think it would bring spirits and demons into our home. So, forgive me for being ignorant of the device."

"Demons and evil spirits are as real as you and I. God speaks of them repeatedly in the Holy Bible as actual spiritual beings, not imaginary, but real. Most spirits reside on what is called the Astral Plane, a plane of existence, crossed by the soul in its astral body on the way to being born and after death. Occult practices such as astrology, tarot cards, and especially spirit boards are means of communicating with those spirits who are trapped in the astral plane. Usually, those spirits died a violent death or committed suicide. A Christian would not venture into such territory. It is against the Word of God."

"Look, I understand what God expects from me and my family. But this accusation that we're practicing occult by conjuring up evil spirits from the astral plane just doesn't make a lick of sense to me."

"Demons have the same rebellious evil nature as Satan himself. They hate God and His creation and seek to destroy it. People are a vulnerable target for demons because mankind was made in God's image and originally had dominion of the Earth. Evil spirits endeavor to lead men and women to sin and enter them to express themselves doing evil."

"As I said, fault us for being ignorant of the use of a spirit board. They sell them at toy stores."

Father McKinley looked up from his briefcase at David. "The Bible also speaks numerously about the assistance of mediums and how it is forbidden in the eyes of the Lord."

"So, what are you saying Father?"

"You were tempted by evil to play the spirit board against God's Will and now you and your family are paying the debts."

David was silent.

"When this is over, you should take a good look at yourself. Are you living the life that God would want you to live? Or are you unconsciously doing the work of the Devil?"

"I mean no disrespect Father, but did you come here for an exorcism or to preach?"

"I've spoken my mind." McKinley opened his bag and retrieved his surplice, consisting of cotton fabric. He put it on. The surplice reached his ankles with wide sleeves and lace inserts. He reached in the bag and took out a bottle of holy water. David's eyes widened. He felt as if he was experiencing a scene from the "Exorcist" movie. The priest turned to David. "It would be wise if you would step out of the house while I conduct the rite," he said.

"You don't have to ask me twice," David said, walking out the front door.

With David outside, Father McKinley gathered his thoughts, took a deep breath and began the exorcism. He nailed a cross on the wall of every room. He walked throughout the house, sprinkling Holy Water on the walls as a form of purification, speaking the Gospel in Latin, almost whispering. Then, after walking into each room of the house, he opened his Bible and began to speak the Word of God in a calm soothing voice while continuing to throw Holy Water against the walls of the possessed trailer.

"And in the name of the Father, the Son, and the Holy Spirit, I cast such demons back to the depths of Hell. Our Lord, strengthened by the intercession of the Immaculate Virgin Mary, Mother of our Savior, of Blessed Michael the Archangel, of the Blessed Apostles Peter and Paul and all the Saints, we confidently undertake to repulse the attacks and deceits of the Devil. God arises; His enemies are scattered and those who hate Him flee before Him. As smoke is driven away, so are they driven; as wax melts before the fire, so the wicked perish at the presence of God."

Father McKinley raised his cross high in the air. "Behold the Cross of the Lord, flee bands of enemies. May thy mercy, Lord, descend upon us."

Upon that statement, the walls began to grumble like the sound of distant thunder. "That's right demons." Father said. "Time to wake up!"

David waited patiently outside, looking into the windows. He could see Father McKinley pacing back and forth in the living room, holding a cross high in the air and dousing Holy Water on the walls. He wanted this nightmare to be over. Perhaps tonight would be the night that it all ends.

The house began to heat up. Father McKinley could feel it. He tugged at his collar to loosen it up a bit and began to speak in a commanding and authoritative voice, with exalted confidence and fervor. He knew he had the demon's attention.

He continued in a commanding voice. "I cast you out, unclean spirit, along with every satanic power of the enemy, every specter from Hell, and all your fell companions; in the name of our Lord Jesus Christ. Begone! For it is He who commands you. He who flung you headlong from the heights of Heaven into the depths of Hell. It is He who commands you. He who once stilled the sea and the wind and the storm. Hearken, therefore, and tremble in fear, Satan, you enemy of the Faith, you foe of the human race, you begotten of death, you robber of life, you corrupter of justice, you root of all evil and vice; seducer of man, betrayer of the nations, instigator of envy, formentor of discard, author of pain and sorrow…"

David stood about thirty feet from the trailer, his heart beating rapidly. He could hear Father McKinley speaking out to the demons. He was nervous, hoping that the demons would be gone after he was done with the rite. He could hear Father talking in a demanding voice, but he couldn't make out what he was saying. Even though he was nervous and scared, he was proud of himself. He had brought the big guns to the fight and the evil was getting it left and right.

Arthur approached the trailer. "David."

"Mr. Rasberry," David replied, surprised. "Now is not a good time."

"On the contrary, it's a perfect time."

David stared at Arthur, perplexed. He noticed Arthur carrying a long bag over his shoulder.

"That priest will need all the help he can get. Are you ready for this?"

David eyed the bag. "Ready for what?"

Father McKinley continued, his voice increasing, his body temperature almost unbearable. "Give place to Christ in whom you have found none of your works; give place to the One, Holy, Catholic, and Apostolic Church acquired by Christ at the price of His blood. Stoop beneath the all-powerful Hand of God; tremble and flee when we invoke the Holy and Terrible Name of Jesus, this Name to which the Virtues, Powers, and Dominations of Heaven are humbly submissive, this Name which causes Hell to tremble."

Just then, Father McKinley lost his balance. He felt the trailer move. David and Arthur couldn't believe it as they watched the trailer rock slightly back and forth. A cinder block gave way and crumbled from the shift. The trailer stopped moving and David and Arthur could hear the priest shouting the Name of God.

Arthur stood in front of David. "We need to go in there and help him before it's too late."

David was in a panic. "What the hell can we do to help?"

"Follow my lead."

McKinley rose to his feet as the hot wind blew inside the trailer. Pictures began to fall from the walls, dishes fell into the floor. The curtains swayed wildly in the wind as Father McKinley, with feet firmly planted, continued in the most commanding tone he could muster. "We drive you from us, unclean spirits, satanic powers, infernal invaders and wicked legions; in the Name and by the power of our Lord Jesus Christ, may you be snatched away and driven from the Church of God and from the souls made to the image and likeness of God and redeemed by the Precious Blood of the Divine Lamb."

Father McKinley felt the trailer move again. He doused Holy Water on the floor; splashed it across the walls. The Holy Water produced steam wherever it landed like it was burning the flesh of the demon itself. The strong heated wind blew through the trailer as the lights began to flicker.

When David opened the front door, it nearly knocked him down as the door blew open from the wind. David could feel the heat against his skin immediately. He turned to Arthur. "On second thought, I think Father McKinley's doing a great job."

Arthur shook his head. "It's time to go in and help."

David and Arthur made their way in, struggling to get down the hall as the hot wind blew against them. They could hear Father McKinley screaming out to the demons.

"The Most High God commands you! The Eternal Son commands you! The Eternal Holy Ghost commands you! Jesus, God's Word made flesh, commands you!"

The wind increased and the air becoming too hot.

Arthur reached behind him. David stared at Arthur who was holding a knife, with scribblings of writings on the blade, the handle made of bone. David grabbed Arthur's hand and hollered, "What the hell is that?"

Father McKinley turned to David and Arthur, waved his hand towards them. "Get out of here!"

Arthur didn't move. David didn't know what to do.

McKinley was finding it difficult to breathe, but he continued, looking up towards the ceiling he continued. "He who built His church on the firm rock and declared that the gates of Hell shall not prevail against her commands you! The Sacred Sign of the Cross commands you!"

Every mirror in the house shattered. The curtains came down at the mercy of the wind. Father McKinley felt his throat close as if someone had a stranglehold on him. He began to cough but continued throwing Holy Water, showing the Cross, and exorcising the demon away. He was determined to finish the rite and send the demon back to Hell. "The power of the mysteries…of the Christian Faith commands you! The Faith of the Holy Apostles Peter and Paul…commands you!"

David was worried. He could hear the trailer grinding on its supports as the Father continued his rite. David noticed that none of the windows had curtains on them. The aluminum windows were rattling. He could see Father McKinley's surplice blowing against the wind.

McKinley stood his ground. "Begone, Satan, inventor and master of all deceit, the enemy of man's salvation. I cast ye down to the depths of Hell!" McKinley doused Holy Water and professed with conviction. "Leave this place! Leave this holy place and return to your eternal damnation!"

Suddenly, Father McKinley felt a tight grip on his throat. Then suddenly the demon appeared in front of him. Father McKinley's eyes widened. David and Arthur stared across the room in shock. It was the one known as Kasdeya! A faint silhouette of the demon poised in front of Father McKinley. The demon's horns were visible, his face blood red, eyes black as darkness.

McKinley grabbed his own throat with both hands, trying to break free of the grip, but he was losing his breath. McKinley rose off the floor; being choked in the air.

"Now David!" Arthur shouted as he ran to the center of the living room, kneeling. "David!" Arthur shouted. "Join me!"

David ran over to Arthur as Arthur pulled out of his bag…the spirit board!

"What the hell!"

The heat of the wind was unbearable. They could barely breathe. Father McKinley was still suspended from the floor in a deathly chokehold.

Arthur screamed at David as he unfolded the board on the floor. "Place your hands around the board."

David did as commanded.

Arthur raised the knife and drove it into the center of the board.

A scream blared throughout the trailer, nearly shattering the windows as Father McKinley dropped to the floor and the wind died. David and Arthur ran to Father McKinley, lying on his back, with red marks around his neck. David could barely breathe from the heat that consumed the room.

David felt his pulse. "He's not breathing!"

25

The ambulance arrived at the hospital with Father McKinley in tow. David was behind them as they stormed through the doors of the emergency room with the priest.

A doctor entered the hall. "What happened?" he asked.

"He was performing an exorcism in my home and he just fell out," David said.

The doctor looked at him in disbelief.

David sighed. "I wouldn't lie about something like that."

"Get him into ICU," the doctor ordered one of the nurses.

He turned to David, holding him back. "You need to wait out here. We'll let you know of his condition."

Before entering the waiting room, David waited by the telephone to call Erica. An elderly man was talking to someone on the other end. He was crying; saying he needed someone to talk to. His little girl was dying. David couldn't help but feel sorry for him, but his own crisis was overshadowing all his emotions. He stood against the cold wall, listening to voices of nurses and doctors in the hallway, a woman's voice over an intercom system, waiting for his turn at the phone. He felt numb all over; the past hour seemed fuzzy as if he'd just woke up from a dream. The damp hospital smell he was inhaling didn't sit too well with his stomach. He always hated hospitals, especially waiting rooms.

The elderly man slowly hung up the phone. David wanted to say something to him. Let him know he was sorry, but he didn't say a word. David lifted the phone and called Erica. He told her what happened to Father

McKinley. It made him feel good to hear Erica's voice. A beautiful sound that brightened up a dimly lit hospital hallway. Erica told David she would leave Billy with her mom and that she was on her way there to join him.

It had been just over an hour when one of the nurses came out of ICU. David and Erica could tell it wasn't good by the look on her face.

"Ok, first of all, he's going to make it," the nurse said with a straining smile. But he's having trouble remembering things," the nurse continued, "due partly from lack of oxygen to his brain. We're hoping that he recovers from that quickly."

"Can we see him?" David asked.

"No," the nurse replied. "Seeing you may make matters worse. You need to give him time to recover."

"There's something very important I need to ask him," David demanded.

"He doesn't even know what day it is," the nurse said. "Much less what just happened to him. The last thing he remembers is leaving the church from preaching."

"Come on David," Erica said, nudging him along. "Let's go for now. Give him time to rest."

e

David and Erica returned home, wondering if it was back to normal. They began putting the curtains back on the walls and sweeping up the broken glass. Erica noticed a different feel in the trailer. "Honey, can you feel that?"

"Feel what?" David asked.

"I don't know. I can't describe it, but it feels different in here; a calmness to it."

"Maybe it's from all the Holy Water and God speak splashed around the house," David said, unconvinced.

"Come on," Erica said, "be positive."

"I thought I was the psychic one in the family," David said with a smile.

"Maybe you're rubbing off on me," Erica replied.

David looked outside and noticed Arthur making his way towards the house.

"Excuse me Erica," David said rushing out the door.

David stepped onto the deck, approaching Arthur. "You left when the ambulance came for Father McKinley. You have some explaining to do."

Arthur drew a long breath. "Yes, I suppose I do."

Erica walked onto the deck, standing next to David's side. "What's going on?"

David turned to Erica. "During the exorcism, Arthur brought over a strange knife and… the spirit board."

Erica turned to Arthur, not replying.

David continued. "When Father McKinley was lifted into the air in a chokehold, Arthur and I rushed into the trailer. Arthur unfolded the board and had me place my hands on it while he drove the knife into the center of the board."

Erica continued staring at Arthur. "I don't know what to say."

Arthur cleared his throat. "Perhaps a little dramatic."

"Perhaps," David replied. "But what kind of plan was that? What was that knife? And how did you get your hands on the board in the first place?"

Arthur stood firm. "Your brother, Richard, was kind enough to help."

"Geez, I bet he was," David replied.

"Regarding the dagger," Arthur said, "it is over 300 years old. The handle is made from the bone of a dead saint and the blade is engraved with the writings of scripture, carved by a Vatican priest. Years ago, my father practiced along the borderlines of witchcraft. He gave that dagger to me right before his passing."

David and Erica made glances at each other.

Arthur continued. "He taught me a few things about dealing with violent spirits. My plan was based on its origin. It was you who brought the board into your home. You had to be the one who's hands rested on it as I plunged the dagger into it. That set in motion the reverse of the evil that had plagued your home. With the help of Father McKinley's exorcism, it was a perfect time. The demon was caught off guard."

"I see," David replied. "I thought you didn't practice in the occult."

"Mr. Chandler, there comes a time in a man's life where he must do what he knows is right, even if it falls against his beliefs. My actions today may come back to haunt me later, but a man's life was saved because of those actions. I take full responsibility."

Erica replied, "Thank you, for what you did today."

David turned to her. "We don't know if our house is safe or not." Turning back to Arthur, he said, "I must thank you as well, Mr. Rasberry. My apologies. But I must ask. How did you know it would work?"

Arthur shook his head. "I didn't."

David scoffed. "We could've all been killed today. You didn't have a good psychic feeling that the plan would work?"

"Nothing of the sort," Arthur replied. "I relied on good old-fashioned faith."

Erica smiled at David. "Well David, you can't argue with that."

"There's something else you should know," Arthur said. "David, I'm sure you know that board belonged to me. I gave it to your father upon his request."

David nodded. "I'm aware of that."

"What you're not aware of was the mess your father got into with that board."

David was startled. "What are you saying?"

"Well, that's for your father to share, not me."

"Then why bring it up?"

Arthur sighed. "After your father was finished with that board, I asked him what he did with it."

David waited patiently for Arthur's response.

"Your father swore to me that he burned it."

David turned to Erica, confused. "My father lied to you?"

Arthur looked away, then back at David and Erica. "For all our sakes, I sure hope so."

～

That evening, David and Erica cuddled on the couch together. They had picked up all the broken glass, put up all the curtains, and arranged the furniture back to its original spots. They were tired and the house was quiet. They sat on the couch, in silence, as the day they experienced played through their heads.

David noticed that Erica was just as quiet, although she didn't witness the same horrible events. She was in distant thought; perhaps thinking heavily about something. The crease between her eyes showed it. "Erica, are you okay?"

Erica looked at David with fear and worry in her eyes. She was troubled by something. "There's something I haven't told you."

David's heart began to beat faster. How could this night get even worse, he thought? "What is it sweetie?" he asked softly.

Erica sipped a glass with water before responding. "I didn't want to tell you this because I was afraid you'd get angry."

David put his arm around her, bringing her closer, he softly replied, "Please tell me."

After a short moment of silence, Erica spoke. "The day I was beginning my painting and Amanda came over, I told you we didn't play the board. I told you that she was against playing it."

"Yes," David replied, swallowing hard. "I remember that day well."

Erica looked down. "I told you that I played the board alone, but I didn't tell you everything."

David drew a long sigh. He placed a hand over his face.

Erica continued. "I asked the board what day I would die. It told me I would die tonight; in my sleep."

David stopped breathing. He quickly looked up at Erica. "Why? Why did you do that?"

"I was stubborn ok? I had to know the answer. It was eating me up inside. I can't explain the feeling. It was as if the board was drawing me into asking the question. I wish I never asked. I know it's not real, but it sure feels real. I feel like tonight is my last night." Tears began to escape her eyes. "I feel like tonight is our last night together. That calmness I'm feeling, what if it's…"

David cut her off. "It's not our last night together sweetie. It's not. The board is lying. It can't tell you when you're going to die or how you're going to die. It just can't."

David got up and took Erica's hand, leading her into the bedroom. They stood near the bed, hugging each other tightly. David brushed her hair with his fingers, trying to erase the horrible thoughts that crossed his mind.

"I love you Erica," David whispered.

"I love you too," Erica said with a sniffle.

They got dressed for bed and laid next to each other, snuggling. The thought of simply holding onto each other just seemed perfect at that moment. They shared memories of their first date, their wedding, and the birth of their son. Erica began to cry more at the thought of not being able to watch Billy grow up. She had said goodbye to Billy before leaving him with her mom. She had kissed her mom goodbye before heading to the hospital to be with David. She wanted to spend the night with her husband, holding onto him as she fell asleep, just in case this was it. The night carried through without a hint of unusual noises, nor strange events. Slowly, they drifted asleep… in each other's arms.

26

David woke up the next morning. The sun shining in his face as he stared out the window. His back was turned to Erica. The thought of her passing quickly devoured him. He didn't want to turn over; he didn't want to face the reality of her passing. His wife. The mother of his child. The love of his life. He wouldn't remarry. He just couldn't envision living the rest of his life with another woman. His heart belonged to Erica. He wanted to cry, but he held up. He turned over quickly to notice Erica was gone!

Confused, David got out of bed and opened the bedroom door. There, standing in front of the stove, was Erica cooking up eggs and bacon for breakfast. She turned to David and gave him a huge smile that, to David, nearly knocked him off his feet.

David rushed to her with arms open and hugged her tightly. "I can't tell you how excited I am right now."

"You?" Erica replied. "What about me? I feel like I cheated death."

David looked into her eyes. "I believe last night was the best sleep I've had in a long time."

"Ditto. Not a creature was stirring."

David grabbed some plates to help Erica. "Speaking of creatures, there's no sign of roaches. I wonder if it's too early to say our house is free of ghosts."

"I'm willing to risk saying it. It's about time for some normal around here, don't you think?"

David replied with a smile. "Today is a new day. A fresh start for us."

"Amen to that," Erica replied. "I thought I'd take the day off from work since I didn't die. I want to spend some time with Billy and my mom this morning. Then, this afternoon, you and I can have some fun of our own." Erica flashed a seductive look.

"Count me in," David replied, smiling ear to ear. "I look forward to that."

⌐

Later that morning, after Erica left to spend time with her mom and Billy, David decided to take it easy and watch TV while sipping on coffee. He began to feel what Erica was describing the night before. It was a feeling of tranquility throughout the house as if everything was finally back to normal. A smile came across David's face as he breathed a sigh of relief. He had been waiting for this day for months.

As David returned from the kitchen with his third cup of coffee, he walked over to the living room window. The window looked out towards the wooded area where David and Richard walked through about a month ago. David peered out the window, looking towards the wooded area, at the trail that he and his brother traveled down. He remembered them finding the area where they built their fort and the old rusty car that belonged to Mr. Rasberry. His thoughts led to Mr. Rasberry's late wife and the board's predictions. He tried to think less about the spirit board and more about the fact that he and Erica were going to be okay; that the worst was over.

Just then, he noticed a deer in the woods, walking parallel with the road. He watched, taking a sip of coffee, as the deer stopped to sniff something on the ground. Then, the deer looked towards the trailer. It was as if the deer was staring straight at David, meeting his gaze. David kept his eyes on the deer. Then suddenly, the deer shot off down the woods, running along the trail. It was as if the

deer saw something that scared him away. David was
startled.

Just then, there was a knock at the back door. David
opened it to see Mr. Rasberry.

"Have you heard from the priest?" Mr. Rasberry asked.
"Is he okay?"

"I'm not sure yet," David replied. "He suffered a slight
concussion from the loss of oxygen to his brain. The nurse
says he'll recover, but when he'll be up for a visit it's
uncertain."

"How are you and Erica doing?" Mr. Rasberry asked.

"We're good," David said with a smile, "considering
what's happened in the last twenty-four hours."

"If I may?" Mr. Rasberry asked, signaling to come in.

"Absolutely," David replied, stepping aside.

Arthur walked in and stood in the living room, looking
around. He was waiting for something. David stared at
him. "Is everything okay, Mr. Rasberry?"

Before David could close the door, Arthur grabbed his
stomach and bent over in severe pain.

"O no!" Mr. Rasberry said. "Not again."

David was shocked. "Mr. Rasberry, you ok?"

"Just get me outside, quickly!" Mr. Rasberry shouted.

David took the old man out towards the shrubs. The
thoughts racing through David's head were not good.
Could the evil still be present inside the house? Surely not.
David stopped at the shrubs.

"What happened in there?" David asked.

"The evil," Arthur said, straining to talk, "is still there. I
could feel it once I was inside." Arthur coughed several
times. "It's just as strong."

David was furious and disappointed. "The plan worked.
We stopped the demon."

Arthur shook his head. "I'm afraid there is still something in your home. I just had to come over to make sure. I'm so sorry David."

David turned back to the trailer. "Not as sorry as I am."

When David returned to the trailer, he got a phone call from Erica. She told David that her uncle dropped by at her mom's place. She hadn't seen her uncle in years. She asked David if he'd like to join them for lunch. David declined and told Erica he was heading over to Richard's to spend time with him. But David had other plans.

◡

When David entered the emergency room, he walked up to the window, asking to see Father McKinley. The nurse directed David to room 112. As David walked down the long hallway, his thoughts were back on the demon and the spirit board again. He hated the fact that their house could still be haunted; that the exorcism didn't work. He wanted answers from the priest. He wanted to hear what he had to say about all this.

The door to room 112 was cracked open. David could hear a TV going in the room. He slowly opened the door, to make sure he didn't have any visitors. No one was there, except Father McKinley, his eyes glued to the TV screen.

"Father?" David whispered.

Father McKinley turned his head towards David, his eyes widened. "David," he said.

"How are you doing?" David asked, sitting in the chair next to McKinley's bed.

"I'm good now," McKinley replied. "I was hoping you'd come by. I've been trying to get them to call you here all morning, but they claim to keep forgetting. They also keep forgetting my jello. I'm dying for some strawberry jello."

David pushed the intercom button next to the bed. The buzzer sounded and a woman's voice blared back. "Yes?"

"Hey, we need some strawberry jello down here in room 112 please."

Father McKinley nodded in appreciation. "My voice is still quite strained from the choking I received."

"You wanted to see me?" David asked.

"Yes David. There's something you need to know if you haven't figured it out yet."

David swallowed hard to avoid choking. "Tell me."

Father McKinley slid up on his bed to get more comfortable. "Your home is still plagued by those demons. And you need to take this seriously. My exorcism and the help from your friend weren't enough to ward off this evil." Father McKinley was almost whispering the words. "What you and your family are dealing with is no ordinary haunted house. An evil demon came through that board while you were playing it and it wants your house. It wants you out."

David dropped his head. "How do you know this?"

"Because I met him!" the priest shouted. He went back to his whispering voice. "I stood in front of him and looked that demon straight in the eyes. He told me that your house belongs to him and that he's not backing down."

"What about the exorcism?"

"I couldn't finish it. You and your friend ended that. That's why this situation is serious. That's why this is no ordinary haunting. In most cases, finishing the rite wipes the house from any evil spirits or demons. Not this one. There's no way I would've finished that rite."

"What can we do now?"

"You must leave your home," the priest demanded. "You pack up your things and get your family out of harm's way and don't look back."

David stood up. "You make it sound simple, but it's not."

Father McKinley grabbed David's arm, pulling him closer. "Listen to me! This isn't a game anymore, you understand? This is a matter of life or death. This demon isn't playing around and soon your family may end up dead…just like the Abbot Brown massacre."

David straightened up. "What do you know about Abbot Brown?"

The priest stared into David's eyes for a moment. "After he killed his family and himself, Rebecca Morris came to me for counsel. I helped her get past all the pain and grief she endured. That girl was broken inside, you hear me. It took help from many people to get her back together after that. I know what happened in that trailer many years ago. And now you've brought Abbot back along with God knows what. That's why I was so eager to help you and your family once I found out from Kristin."

David stood in silence next to the Father's bed.

"The best thing for you to do is pack up and move to another home. Cut your losses and start over. If not, you put your family's lives at risk as well as yourself. Give the demon what he wants. Save your family."

‿

As David left the hospital, he couldn't get Father McKinley's words out of his head. *"Give the demon what he wants."* The idea of letting the demon win didn't sit too well with David for he was stubborn. He knew that he and

Erica worked very hard for many years to finally get a house of their own. Now he must let it go…to a demon?

ç

Everything was quiet that day and into the evening as Erica returned home from her mom's. She brought Billy back with her. Erica hadn't asked David how Richard was doing. She had many stories to tell David about her uncle Charlie who lives in North Dakota. David didn't bother to bring up his visit with the priest. Why? For one thing, he promised Erica they wouldn't talk about demons or spirits in the home. And on the other hand, he didn't feel like rehashing the day with a scared deer, Mr. Rasberry's visit, and Father McKinley telling David to give up their home to the demon. Spending the evening with Erica would be a terrific ending to a horrible day. And so, it was.

ç

2:00 AM

David and Erica were asleep in their bed. Billy was in his bed. A light breeze began to blow into Billy's bedroom. Billy began to toss and turn. His nightlight flickered; the sound of footsteps proceeded towards his bed.

Billy woke up, slowly opening his eyes. He turned over to the edge of the bed and was staring into a pair of red eyes. The demon was standing beside Billy's bed, hovering over, staring at him. Billy continued his stare into the red eyes, thinking he was dreaming. But he wasn't.

Then, the demon spoke. His voice was an echo as if he was speaking inside a tunnel. It was a ghostly reverberating sound, almost hypnotizing.

Billy slowly made his way out of bed. He walked slowly down the hallway. He could feel the demon's hand pressing against his back, guiding him along. The demon motioned Billy to keep moving, towards the front door. When he made it to the door, Billy could hear the demon unlocking it. The chain fell, hitting against the aluminum frame and the door swung open.

Billy began walking down the stairs, and out into the yard. The demon stayed back, watching Billy walk slowly towards the road. As Billy was walking, he heard the door shut behind him. He kept walking. Doing what he was told. He was heading towards the dark eerie forest of pines; towards the narrow dirt trail leading into darkness.

2:12 AM

Erica awoke suddenly, feeling a chill run down her spine. She looked over at David who was covered up to his neck, snoring. Erica eased out of bed to check the thermostat. When she got into the kitchen, she was amazed at the roaches that had returned in full force. She looked over at the thermostat; it was sitting on seventy-five. How strange. Why is it so cold in the house?

She reached over to get a glass, killing some roaches along the way. She cleaned it out, filled it up with water, and drank every drop. She reminded herself to let David know about the roaches first thing in the morning. She turned off the kitchen light and began making her way back to bed. Then, suddenly, she decided to check in on Billy since she was already up. She made her way into the hallway. When she opened the door to his bedroom, she almost fainted at what she didn't see.

"David!" she screamed out in terror. David was up and running into the kitchen before his brain even knew he was awake. "Erica! Erica! What is it?"

When David reached Billy's bedroom, he saw what Erica was looking at. Billy's bed was perfectly made. The sheets were tucked in and the pillow centered in the bed as if no one had slept there the whole night.

Frantically, David and Erica searched the house over. The front and back doors were locked, so they knew he hadn't gone outside. They called out to their son but no response. Erica was crying hysterically. She had just put him to bed just hours ago and now he's missing.

Suddenly, David began to think about what Father McKinley told him. *"This demon isn't playing around and soon your family may end up dead."* David remembered the deer, running scared after looking at the trailer. He remembered looking towards the wooded area that morning, staring down the beaten trail. What was the purpose of that? David turned to Erica.

"Billy isn't in the house," David said. "He's outside and I think I know where."

David and Erica headed for the door, unlocked it but the knob wouldn't turn.

"What the hell?" David said, trying to open the door. "It's stuck!"

"David, do something," Erica shouted.

"Can't you see I'm trying? It's like the door is sealed shut!"

David forcefully tried breaking the door down, ramming into it with his body strength, but no luck. "We're trapped in here."

Erica went to the back door. But it was sealed tight. "What's going on?"

David entered the living room. "It's that damn demon! Kasdeya. He's got us locked in here."

Giving up on the door, Erica turned to David. "We have to do something. Billy is in danger!"

David looked up towards the ceiling. "Listen to me you demon. Kasdeya. Is this your way of getting us out of our house? Huh? Is this your way of getting us to move out? To put our son outside and seal us in? Well, it worked. You win. The house is yours. Now let us out to find our son."

Erica was crying, listening to David shout at the top of his lungs. "I don't know if this is working."

"You win Kasdeya!" David continued shouting. "The house is yours. We give up. But we want our son back. Open the damn doors now!"

The demon wasn't responding.

Erica stormed out of the living room.

David grabbed the phone and called Richard. "Richard, it's David. Billy is missing and we're trapped inside the trailer."

"Hey," Richard replied, "hang on. I'm jumping into my pants now. Heading your way bro."

Just then, Erica came running back into the living room with a baseball bat.

"This shit has got to stop!" Erica shouted as she shattered the windows with one swing of the bat. She broke out the remainder of the glass and jumped out. David, feeling a little embarrassed, grabbed two flashlights and was behind her.

The search for their son was on. They called out to him. Shouting his name. He was nowhere to be found. Erica held on to the bat for protection just in case. She knew it wasn't a kidnapper who took Billy because the doors were still locked. It had to be the work of Kasdeya.

"Erica!" David yelled out. "I'm going into the woods."

David followed the beaten trail, shining his flashlight through the thick pine forest. He called out to Billy but no response.

Erica made her way to the abandoned house next door, calling out to her son. She was desperate. Her next move was to let Mr. Rasberry know and call the police.

Richard pulled up into their driveway. He stormed out of the truck with a shotgun in tow. He saw Erica coming from the abandoned home. "Erica, where's David?"

"He went into the woods! Down that beaten trail."

"David," Richard called out as he made his way into the woods. Erica was heading towards Arthur Rasberry's home when suddenly, she heard David shouting her name.

"Erica!" David shouted.

Erica could barely hear him. He must have been deep into the woods. She rushed towards the start of the beaten trail.

Richard hollered out, "David, you found Billy?"

By the time Erica got there, she heard the most beautiful sound of all. Billy's voice. Talking to his dad. Erica began crying tears of joy as she waited underneath the dimly lit street lamp. Waiting for David to bring him back to safety and into her arms.

David and Richard appeared from the pine thicket, David carrying Billy in his arms. Erica gasped for breath. She ran to meet them at the start of the trail. She grabbed Billy, holding him tightly in her arms. She thought she'd lost him forever, but the warmth of his body against hers subsided those horrible thoughts.

"Are you ok Billy?" Erica asked, looking him over.

"He'll be fine," David replied. "Just some scratches on his bare feet. I found him in a ditch. He must've fallen in it during his walk."

"What happened to you sweetie?" Erica asked, looking into Billy's sleep eyes.

"Yeah," Richard said, "that's what I'd like to know."

Billy wiped tears from his eyes. "This skeleton told me to get out of bed and walk outside," Billy said to his mom.

Erica turned to David, who was furious beyond comprehension.

Billy continued. "The skeleton had red eyes, mommy. He was scary."

"I'm so sorry baby," Erica said, hugging him again. "Mommy should've kept her eyes on you better." Tears ran down her cheeks again.

"I don't want to go back in the house again mommy," Billy said.

Erica looked up at David.

Richard put his hand on David's shoulder. "Pam and I got plenty of room for y'all tonight. Come stay with us."

David and Erica looked back at the trailer as the front door slammed itself shut. David sighed, albeit a feeling of relief.

"Don't worry buddy," David replied, "we won't be going back in there again."

David slowly raised his head to gaze at the trailer once more. All the anger he had built up inside of him for the demon that nearly killed Billy this night would have to subside without revenge. It wasn't worth it. His family meant more to him than anything in the world. He had brought the spirit board inside their home; he had played the board; he was responsible for the resurrection of the evil spirits. If only he'd left the board inside the dark, dusty shed that day he found it. How different would things be at this moment? He had started it and he would end it. The war was over. The demons had won. The trailer belongs to them now.

Epilogue
Two Months Later

David and Erica drove up to Richard and Pam's place. As David and Erica got out of the truck, Richard and Pam met them halfway. Billy went running to Pam as she swooped him up off the ground, hugging him tightly.

"Rich," David said, "you sounded urgent over the phone. What's going on?"

Richard was grinning ear to ear. "I'll let Pam tell you bro," Richard replied, looking over at Pam.

She put Billy down and with one breath she shouted. "I'm pregnant!"

David and Erica lit up with surprise and excitement. Erica went over to Pam and hugged her.

"Congratulations Pam!" Erica said. "I'm so happy for you."

David smiled at his brother, extending his hand. "Congrats Rich," David said. "I knew it would work out for you two someday. You deserve every bit of joy that comes your way."

"Thanks bro," Richard replied. "I can't tell you how happy I am right now. It's a feeling I hope never goes away."

David turned to look at Erica and Billy. His family. "Trust me. It doesn't."

The four of them celebrated Pam's pregnancy by going out that evening for dinner, which was all on David. His father had given him enough money to move into an apartment temporarily while they searched for another home to buy. They sold the trailer for a few hundred dollars to a trailer collector, who sells them for scrap metal or to hunting camps. David told the collector to make sure he sells it as scrap. David's original plan was to burn the trailer to the ground and have a BBQ outing, but the five hundred dollars he received for it will help in providing for his family along with the money his father gave him.

℮

The next morning, David and Erica sat outside on the tailgate of David's truck, eating fried chicken, and watching the movers jack up the haunted trailer.

Erica turned to David. "So, when are you gonna buy me my own set of wheels?" Erica asked with a toothy grin.

"Well, what do I get in return?" David hinted.

Erica gave David that seductive look that he always loves to see.

David couldn't help but smile. "You're amazing," he said, looking into her beautiful eyes. "You know, I'm looking forward to just relaxing for the rest of the day with Billy. Maybe we can play a board game or something."

Then, David caught on to what he just said. He turned to Erica whose facial expression was far from what it was just seconds ago.

"I meant, perhaps, Monopoly," David said, being specific.

"That's much better," Erica said with a smile.

They watched as the big semi-truck drove off their lot with the haunted trailer in tow.

David turned to Erica. "You gonna take a picture?"

"No," Erica replied. "This isn't a memory I want to remember."

℮

The spirit board rested on the top shelf in the dusty old junk shed, where it was to remain for eternity; never to be touched by human hands again. Whether that becomes its fate…is yet to be determined.

～

As the big semi-truck bears down the highway with a police escort in front of it, a minivan catches up.

"Can you pass it Herb?" the woman in the passenger seat asked.

"I reckon not Edna," Herb replied. "I can't seem to get a chance at it."

"Well, we're gonna be late," Edna replied. "Just like last year's reunion."

"You're gonna start that again?"

"Look, Grandma!" A boy shouted from the back seat, pointing towards the trailer. "Look at that man in the window."

The boy's grandparents strained their necks, looking into the far back bedroom window of the trailer house in front of them.

"What man, Peter?" Edna asked. "I don't see any man. Do you Herb?"

"No," Herb replied, "can't say that I do. Unless my bifocals are acting up on me again."

"He's right there," Peter said. "He's staring right at us."

"Peter," Edna said, "sit down before we get pulled over. That's all we need is another ticket."

"Which wasn't my fault by the way," Herb replied.

"Keep telling yourself that," Edna said. "if it helps you sleep at night."

Peter kept staring at the window. "He's right there in the window grandma. He looks like my green army man."

Donny Stephens is an author/publisher living in North Louisiana who self-published his first novel, "Obsession", a young adult mystery/suspense. He is a graduate of Louisiana Tech University where he earned a bachelor's degree in Business Administration/Accounting.

For the latest news and updates, visit and like his page:

www.facebook.com/ Donny Stephens, author

www.ingramcontent.com/pod-product-compliance
Lightning Source LLC
Chambersburg PA
CBHW060133130626
46556CB00006B/2333